DON PENDLETON'S
THE EXECUTIONER®
FEATURING MACK BOLAN®
CUTTING EDGE

D0001926

A GOLD EAGLE BOOK FROM
WORLDWIDE®

TORONTO • NEW YORK • LONDON • PARIS
AMSTERDAM • STOCKHOLM • HAMBURG
ATHENS • MILAN • TOKYO • SYDNEY

First edition July 1990

ISBN 0-373-61139-0

Special thanks and acknowledgment to
Jerry VanCook for his contribution to this work.

Montoya was about to escape

Bolan cut the wheel hard to the left and bore down on the nose of the aircraft, his finger crushing into the trigger button, sending a steady stream of .50-caliber projectiles tearing across the runway.

For a brief moment it seemed as if the jeep and airplane would collide, then the Boeing rose over Bolan's head, its heavy vacuum jerking the machine gun from his grip.

He watched as the plane headed east before dipping a wing and circling back toward the airport. In the light of the full moon, he saw a tiny speck descend through the sky as the Boeing continued out over the Atlantic.

The object grew larger as it neared the ground, finally allowing Bolan to distinguish the outlines of a body.

As the horrifying reality set in, Bolan heard the scream.

Janie Brewer hit the runway fifty feet in front of the Executioner.

MACK BOLAN®

The Executioner

We, too, born to freedom, and believing in freedom, are willing to fight to maintain freedom. We, and all others who believe as deeply as we do, would rather die on our feet than live on our knees.

—Franklin Delano Roosevelt
June 19, 1941

I've been asked, on occasion, what payment I expect for services rendered. Payment? I've been paid, all right, but not in money. The U.S. has provided me and other Americans with the finest brand of freedom in the history of the human race. It's the only payment I've ever gotten. It's the only payment I want.

—Mack Bolan

THE
MACK BOLAN®
LEGEND

Nothing less than a war could have fashioned the destiny of the man called Mack Bolan. Bolan earned the Executioner title in the jungle hell of Vietnam.

But this soldier also wore another name—Sergeant Mercy. He was so tagged because of the compassion he showed to wounded comrades-in-arms and Vietnamese civilians.

Mack Bolan's second tour of duty ended prematurely when he was given emergency leave to return home and bury his family, victims of the Mob. Then he declared a one-man war against the Mafia.

He confronted the Families head-on from coast to coast, and soon a hope of victory began to appear. But Bolan had broken society's every rule. That same society started gunning for this elusive warrior—to no avail.

So Bolan was offered amnesty to work within the system against terrorism. This time, as an employee of Uncle Sam, Bolan became Colonel John Phoenix. With a command center at Stony Man Farm in Virginia, he and his new allies—Able Team and Phoenix Force—waged relentless war on a new adversary: the KGB.

But when his one true love, April Rose, died at the hands of the Soviet terror machine, Bolan severed all ties with Establishment authority.

Now, after a lengthy lone-wolf struggle and much soul-searching, the Executioner has agreed to enter an "arm's-length" alliance with his government once more, reserving the right to pursue personal missions in his Everlasting War.

1

The house reeked of death, the death of the thousands who had died so that it might be built.

Mack Bolan raised the bottle of beer to his lips, took a sip and carefully returned it to the coaster on the coffee table. The clink of glass against glass echoed hollowly throughout the spacious room. Bolan's eyes scanned the oak-paneled walls of the second-story den, the warrior's mind instinctively registering possible cover, concealment and escape routes that might be utilized at a moment's notice. Leaning back in the overstuffed leather armchair, he crossed his legs and felt the Beretta 93-R bite into the hard flesh beneath his belt.

Mexico meant hot weather; hot weather meant no jackets and no jackets meant no holsters—at least not in the role he was playing.

Once again he took inventory of the wooden gun cabinet on the far wall: three bolt-action hunting rifles, one 12-gauge Ithaca shotgun and an Uzi. Some or all of which he might soon call into action.

His decision to go undercover into one of the largest of the Medellín cartels had left him necessarily undergunned.

Absently Bolan studied the label on the Mexican beer bottle before him, mentally retracing the steps that had led him to the Rodriguez ranch. David Warren, the cartel's new American connection, had finally agreed to tell Bolan all he knew about the pickup scheduled today at this ranch house south of Nuevo Laredo. A special little Executioner interrogation had convinced Warren it was his only course of action.

Bolan had learned from Warren that this Mexican faction of the Colombia-based cartel had never met the American face-to-face. The warrior had decided to simply step in and take his place, and the American death merchant was given a one-way ticket to the hell he so richly deserved.

The Executioner surveyed the elaborate den once more, knowing his unease stemmed from the fact that it had all gone too smoothly. So far, waiting had proved to be the hardest part of the mission. The cocaine shipment from Colombia wouldn't arrive until evening, and it went against the Executioner's grain to lounge around a multimillion-dollar ranch house built by the blood of others.

He suddenly became alert, his senses detecting the rich smell of a cigar that would cost the average Mexican peasant a week's pay. Seconds later the heavily carved oak door to the hall swung open on silent hinges.

Manuel Rodriguez waddled into the room and set a silver tray of caviar, fruit and assorted cheeses on the coffee table before collapsing into the sofa across from Bolan. Smoke streamed from an enormous Cuban cigar caressed by the Mexican's fleshy lips. The thin, light blue cloth of the fancy pleated *guayabera* rode up his side, revealing rolls of fat that folded the top of his slacks over the restricting alligator belt. Contentment oozed from the drug dealer as he settled into the soft leather upholstery and blew a perfect smoke ring toward the rough-hewn ceiling beams.

"So, Señor Warren," Rodriguez finally said, "how shall we spend our day? I have an excellent bottle of tequila in the cabinet. Scotch or cognac, if you prefer." He paused to lean forward to the coffee table, his face reddening with the exertion. Heaping caviar onto a huge slab of white cheese, he jammed it past his lips, tiny black eggs falling from the sides of his mouth to leave purple stains on the front of his shirt. "I have also several of the most beautiful young women in all Mexico here today," Rodriguez continued through the mouthful of food. "And as you Americans like to joke, each of them a virgin." The giant belly quivered as he cackled with vulgar laughter.

Bolan lifted his Corona and smiled. "I'm fine."

"Yes, though we have never met, we have many common friends. They tell me you're a man of restraint. I like that. I like that very much. I think this is the beginning of a very long and profitable friendship of our own."

The Executioner smiled once more, careful not to show his impatience. "I'm sure that it is."

Bolan was sure that the next few hours would be profitable. Not to Rodriguez, or the cartel, but to the decent citizens of the world. As soon as the plane carrying the cocaine arrived, he would take care of the ruthless savage and the rest of his men, destroy the shipment, then search the ranch for leads that would take him to the next rung on the cartel's ladder.

The warrior leaned back once more in the armchair. He smiled again at his host, this time without strain. "Yes, Señor Rodriguez, I'm sure that today will be profitable."

It was then that they heard the plane.

Rodriguez smiled. "Ah, amigo. It seems that your order arrives early." The fat man struggled from the couch and waddled toward the large picture window overlooking the courtyard and landing strip.

Bolan followed. Far in the distance he saw a speck grow larger as it neared the ranch. Soon the distinctive lines of a Beechcraft Baron became visible. From the corner of his eye, he saw wrinkles of curiosity begin to etch across Rodriguez's face.

"That's not our airplane," Rodriguez said.

Bolan turned to face him. "Then whose is it?"

Rodriguez shrugged, turned his palms up and extended his arms in Latin drama. "I don't know." Turning suddenly toward Bolan, he asked suspiciously, "How about you, *señor*? Do you know who is honoring me with a surprise visit?"

"No," Bolan stated flatly.

The Executioner's eyes followed Rodriguez to the telephone on the bar. One hand lifted the receiver from its cradle while the pudgy fingers of the other tapped numbers. The man spoke in rapid Spanish, and through the window Bolan saw half a dozen men, armed with Uzis and M-16s, gather near the elaborately landscaped courtyard.

Rodriguez replaced the telephone. "It's undoubtedly nothing, Señor Warren. Perhaps a pilot who has gone off course and needs directions. It happens with small aircraft." Rodriguez stuffed a new cigar in his mouth and lighted it. "But in our business," he said through puffs of black smoke, "it pays to take no chances, eh? I have alerted my guards here as well as the reinforcements who are presently waiting to protect your shipment tonight. They will arrive early—just in case."

Bolan glanced again at the gun cabinet on the wall behind him. Depending on who was in the plane that now circled overhead, he might need its contents earlier than he'd planned.

Rodriguez rejoined Bolan at the window as the Beechcraft prepared to land, coughing and choking, with bluish-green clouds of smoke trailing behind.

The dealer seemed relieved. "Ah, amigo," he said. "As you see, I was correct. It appears one of the engines is out, no?"

"No." The Executioner didn't know who was in the plane that now touched down on the landing strip, didn't know if it was friend or foe. But years of doing battle in the jungles of southeast Asia—and those created by drug pushers and other savages throughout the world—had honed Bolan's instinct for impending trouble to a razor's edge.

Regardless of who exited the airplane in the next few moments, Bolan knew that a firefight was about to take place.

Without speaking, he drew the Beretta from beneath his waistband and smashed the weapon against the temple of the flabby-faced dealer.

Before the drug lord's body hit the floor, the warrior was on the move, crossing the room to reach the gun cabinet. He grabbed both the Uzi and Ithaca 12-gauge, slung the shotgun over his shoulder and returned the Beretta to his waistband along with extra magazines for the Uzi.

He got back to the window just in time to see four heavily armed men in black vests and hoods exit the plane, firing on the run. Two of Rodriguez's drug guards went down while the others scrambled for cover.

Still wondering who the new arrivals might be, Bolan raced down the steps of the ranch house. On the landing halfway to the bottom, a surprised and confused guard raised a .357 Magnum as Bolan approached.

He was a split second too slow.

Firing from the hip, the Executioner cut a 9 mm S from the gunner's waist to his neck.

Through the glass doors to the courtyard, Bolan saw two of the newcomers sprint across the runway toward the hangar. The steady fire of the other two had the remaining Mexican gunners pinned down behind various cover. Closer now, Bolan could see that the black headgear the invaders wore extended down over their faces to form a mask.

Bolan's gut-level instinct told him that the men in the ski masks were no better than the savages who returned their fire. But while the Executioner had learned to trust his instincts, he had always gone to whatever extent was necessary to ensure the safety of innocents. Anyone on the side of justice—police, military, even morally justified mercenaries—were his allies.

Even when they mistakenly hunted him. Even when they tried to kill him.

And Bolan wasn't positive that the newcomers were the enemy. Any number of possibilities existed, ranging from American DEA agents to rival drug dealers. True, their disguises suggested motives less than honorable, but the Executioner wouldn't act until he was certain.

Bolan had never killed an innocent man, and he wasn't about to start now. But as he burst through the glass doors to the courtyard, the warrior *was* sure that this Mexican branch of the Medellín cocaine empire was the enemy. So he'd focus his attention on them. And if he learned in the process that these mysterious new arrivals were yet another threat to the law-abiding citizens of the world then they, too, would feel the cleansing fire of the Executioner.

Raising the Uzi, Bolan fired a long burst at a cartel gunner who'd taken refuge behind a concrete statue of Aphrodite. The first few rounds shattered the Greek goddess, and Bolan heard the hidden man's screams as concrete exploded around him.

The final rounds of the burst silenced those screams.

One of the intruders dropped to one knee on the runway and fired a battle-scarred Thompson at a fleeing figure behind the swimming pool pump house. The other masked man struggled furiously with a weapon malfunction.

Bolan dived headfirst behind a large planter and watched as the clumsy man, hands fumbling with an M-16, took a round in the chest. The force knocked him to his back, but he was on his feet again in seconds, still trying vainly to clear a jammed cartridge from the M-16's ejection port.

Bolan took a closer look at the man's black vest. Kevlar. The helmet and face mask were undoubtedly made from the same bullet-resistant material.

The Executioner fired another burst as the man with the jammed weapon took two rounds in the knee from a gunner who'd suddenly appeared on the roof. Bolan raised the Uzi and caught the sniper with a short burst to the throat. The man tumbled forward, his foot catching in the gutter at the roof's edge and somersaulting him into the swimming pool below.

Bolan sprang to his feet and dashed toward what remained of the statue of Aphrodite. Spitting his own cover fire as he ran, the Executioner dived over the body under the shattered concrete and rolled to a stop behind another, similar structure.

Ares. Greek god of war.

From this new vantage point, he could see the hangar on the other side of the runway where the two men who'd crossed earlier now taxied a small Cessna through the overhead door.

Bolan shoved a fresh clip into the Uzi and crouched behind the edge of the statue, inching his way into position to take out the remaining guards who lay hidden behind a three-foot brick wall. Suddenly two hands lifted an AK-47 over the bricks and fired blindly in the direction of both Bolan and the newcomers on the tarmac. The warrior ducked behind cover. He dropped the Uzi and unslung the Ithaca, racking the slide to chamber a round. Pressing the stock firmly against his right shoulder, he cut loose two rounds of double-aught buckshot. The AK-47 tumbled out of sight beneath the brick.

The second gunner behind the wall rose and fired his Uzi at the masked men on the runway, effectively stopping what appeared to be a halfhearted attempt by the Thompson-gunner to drag his wounded partner to safety. Several rounds went wild, cutting through the thin skin of the Beechcraft Baron, and Bolan heard the man with the Thompson curse as the pilot took off down the runway to escape the onslaught.

The Executioner fired his third round of buckshot through the embroidered peasant shirt of the Mexican gunner behind the wall. Wild eyes rolled up and under the lids as the corpse plunged forward over the bricks.

From the corner of his eye, Bolan saw the man with the Thompson bolt across the runway toward the

Cessna, twisting periodically to lay down short bursts. Some of the rounds flew toward the ranch house, but the fleeing masked man directed most of his fire at his fallen comrade on the runway.

From somewhere far in the distance came the faint sound of vehicles approaching the ranch.

Rodriguez's reinforcements.

The Executioner had no idea how many men he might face when they arrived in the next few minutes. Checking his weaponry, he counted one shell left in the low-capacity Ithaca and two full clips for the Uzi. And the Beretta didn't have a full magazine.

It wouldn't be enough. Not by a long shot.

Bolan harbored no fear of death. He had resigned himself to its dark embrace long ago when he first embarked on his one-man war against evil. He fought each battle under the assumption that he was already dead, in a sense, and that each breath he took, each shot he fired, was on borrowed time. But he had vowed that as many as possible of the world's human predators would accompany him down that lonely dark road.

The warrior quickly scanned the ranch house. He could retrace his steps and procure the remaining weapons and ammunition in the upstairs gun cabinet, but bolt-action rifles were hardly what this situation warranted, and his quick inventory had revealed a very limited supply of ammo for the Uzi and shotgun. The ranch's primary arsenal had to be hidden somewhere on the grounds, but he'd need time to locate it.

And time was something the Executioner didn't have.

This arm of the cartel was only a small part of a virus that threatened to infect the world. Many other, larger wars remained to be fought. If his quest ended here, the plague would rage on, eventually engulfing society.

Bolan gritted his teeth as he made a decision that tore at his soul. He wouldn't, *couldn't*, sacrifice the war for one battle. Withdrawal was the only sensible course of action.

Temporary withdrawal. He'd return to his shabby hotel room in Nuevo Laredo to regroup and rearm.

And return.

Bolan replaced the near-empty Uzi chip with a fresh one. Far in the distance he could see the masked man with the Thompson grab the door of the taxiing Cessna and swing on board.

A short, muscular Mexican rose from behind the brick wall and took his time sighting on the Cessna, which gave the Executioner more than enough time of his own to take out the man with a stream of 9 mm death.

Bolan raced back into the ranch house and down the hall to the front door. As he exited onto the front porch, he was greeted by a burst of fire from the first wave of reinforcements. Diving through the now-shredded porch screen, he hit the ground on his left shoulder, rolled, then ducked behind the cover of the concrete steps. A Cadillac Seville skidded to a halt not ten feet away.

The driver was no fool. He threw the transmission into reverse and angled the car, the Caddie's mammoth engine block separating him from Bolan as he got out on the opposite side.

But the man in the passenger seat sat exposed like a sacrificial lamb. Bolan saw the realization spread across the hood's face. His tight mouth widened into a silent O as he desperately brought up both hands in a futile attempt to block the parabellums that ripped through his fingers and into his face.

A dozen more cartel vehicles approached in a storm of dust. The warrior had only moments before he'd be surrounded by countless gunners, better armed than he and lusting for revenge.

The driver of the Cadillac hadn't fired a shot and seemed content to ride out the standoff until assistance arrived. Bolan knew that in less than a minute the convoy would navigate the pit-ridden road and be on him.

Rising from behind the steps, the Executioner showered the remainder of his final magazine over the hood of the Cadillac, carefully avoiding the car itself. He dropped the empty weapon and ripped the Beretta from his waistband as he rolled forward and under the Caddie. He came to rest beneath the car, on his stomach, the 93-R clutched in a two-handed grip and aimed at the exposed legs of the driver.

Firing low, Bolan caught the guy with a 3-round burst to the ankles, knocking his feet from under him and sending him sprawling and screaming to the dirt.

Dust flew into the Executioner's nose and eyes as the Beretta spit a second burst through the man's head.

The warrior slid from beneath the Caddie and dived into the open door next to the dead man. The engine was still running, and he slammed the transmission into drive, cutting a hard U toward the oncoming cavalry.

The Caddie didn't have the speed he would have liked, but it would have to do. It was the only game in town.

Bolan forced himself to drive slowly toward the convoy, the near-empty Beretta held tightly in his left hand and concealed beneath the car window. He would be relying on surprise and the hope that the arriving gunmen had been too far away to see the details of what had actually transpired in front of the house.

It worked. Recognizing the Cadillac, the driver of the lead vehicle slowed as Bolan approached, his face concealed behind the sun visor. With his left thumb, the Executioner flipped the Beretta's safety to semiauto to conserve his remaining ammo.

Bolan pulled casually off the road and alongside the first car as if to speak to the driver. Inching slowly to a crawl, he raised the Beretta as the other driver came to a halt.

He saw the shock in the man's eyes as the angle of view changed, and the Executioner's face was revealed behind the sun visor.

Bolan squeezed lightly on the trigger and the 93-R spit two 9 mm projectiles into the surprised Mexican's forehead, forming a second set of eyes above the brows.

Dirt and gravel showered the vehicles as Bolan floored the accelerator. As he passed the second, idling car, he snapped a shot into the left front tire. By the time he'd reached the third vehicle in the line, the surprised occupants had had time to react. Bolan took out another front tire, then ducked beneath the rush of lead that blew over him, shattering the windshield and sending shards of glass stinging into his skin.

Cutting the wheel hard to the right, the Executioner fired a round into the tire of the next car, then set off across the pasture. Cactus flew from the Caddie's bumper, the pieces exploding across the hood and in through the open windshield.

In the rearview mirror, he counted eight remaining Jeeps, station wagons and luxury cars. And if the vehicles he'd already encountered were any indication, each would contain at least two well-armed gunmen.

A hard smile crossed Bolan's lips as he watched in the mirror. As he'd hoped, the enemy was dividing. Two Jeeps and one station wagon pulled from the road in pursuit as the remaining operable vehicles continued toward the ranch house to investigate.

Three cars.

How many men?

Bolan caught sight of the canyon at the last minute. Stomping hard on the Caddie's brake pedal, he jerked the wheel to the left, skidding to a 180-degree stop through a whirlwind of dirt and disintegrating cactus. The dead body next to him bobbed furiously against the restraint of the seat belt, launching drops of blood against what was left of the windshield.

By the time the vehicle had come to a full stop, inches from the sixty-foot drop, the lead Jeep was no more than two-hundred yards away.

Bolan twisted the ignition key, trying vainly to ignite the stalled engine before leaping from the vehicle and racing toward the canyon.

The first wave of gunfire drove puffs of sand and dirt into the air around the Executioner's legs as he zig-zagged toward the lip of the canyon. Ten yards from the edge, he plunged headfirst to the ground, rolling onto his back to face the Jeep as he slid.

The vehicle slowed as it neared the rim, and from where he lay, Bolan squinted down the barrel of the Beretta. In the distance he could see the other Jeep, followed closely by the station wagon.

The warrior rested the Beretta's front sight on the chest of the man riding shotgun as he attempted to level an Ingram MAC-11. Tugging gently on the trigger, the Executioner's next to last shot blew through the man's ragged T-shirt, exploding the heart beneath.

The driver had his hands full as he urged the Jeep over the pasture's rugged terrain, but he twisted sideways in his seat and reached for something behind him.

The Beretta barked its final round, which entered the driver's head near his left ear and exited near the right, half the man's head following in its wake.

Bolan was on his feet and running toward the vehicle before the body had slumped in the seat, blood soaked legs trapped beneath the dashboard. Prying the Ingram from the passenger's death grip, he turned toward the second Jeep and cut a figure eight from passenger to driver as return fire sang past his head.

The driver fell forward on the accelerator, which rocketed the 4x4 toward the canyon wall. Two gunners leaped from the back seat and fired as Bolan dived over the first vehicle. The Jeep continued its death march to the canyon and plummeted over the edge, exploding on impact.

The Executioner drilled two rounds each into the men on the ground before hearing the dull metal thud as the Ingram's bolt locked open. Dropping the useless piece of iron, he leaned over the driver of the vehicle and saw what the man had been reaching for in the seconds before his death—an Ithaca. Four rounds, five, max. *If* one was already chambered.

There was no time to check.

Bolan wished fleetingly for the Desert Eagle, the mammoth .44 Magnum that he'd left in the hotel room in Nuevo Laredo. Then pushing such unproductive intrusions from his mind, he racked the slide of the Ithaca. A red-cased deer slug fell uselessly from the bottom of the weapon as the station wagon skidded to a halt twenty yards away.

The Executioner ducked under the Jeep and rolled to his right, firing as he rounded the vehicle's rear wheel. He felt the reassuring recoil against his shoulder as a 12-gauge slug tore through the station wagon's hood amid a deluge of water from the radiator.

He rolled back left, taking cover once more and pumping another slug into the Ithaca's chamber. Automatic fire kept him in place until he heard the distinctive sound of an empty M-16 magazine ejecting. Rolling to his right this time, Bolan sent a slug smashing into the face of the driver as he attempted to force a fresh clip into the weapon.

Suddenly aware that he was now alone, the last gunner vaulted from the station wagon and ran back toward the ranch house. Bolan let him go.

The warrior wiped the sweat and grime from his forehead with his shirt sleeve. Dropping the shotgun into the back seat of the lead Jeep, he walked slowly around the vehicle, opened the door and pulled the lifeless driver from behind the wheel.

It was then that he smelled the gasoline and saw the bullet hole through which the pungent fluid dripped before settling in a pool on the ground.

One Jeep with a hole in the gas tank. One station wagon with a demolished radiator. And his third means of transportation still on fire at the bottom of the canyon.

Bolan shielded his eyes with his hand as he peered across the pasture at the tiny figures scurrying around the ranch house. They'd had more than enough time to assess the situation and would now be setting off to assist in Bolan's pursuit.

It was a good twenty-mile walk to Nuevo Laredo, a long walk, Bolan thought, through canyons, cactus and desert.

The Executioner smiled wearily as he made his way down the steep wall of the canyon toward the burning Jeep and the rugged, confusing terrain beyond.

A long walk, maybe. A shorter run.

He heard the first vehicle halt overhead. It looked like he'd have company.

2

Bolan held the empty Beretta in his hand as he dashed toward the nearest thicket of shrubs. Left unsecured in his waistband, there was too great a chance that the gun could drop out as he ran.

And even round-dry, the 93-R was never useless.

He passed the burning vehicle, the stench of simmering flesh rank in his nostrils, and took cover behind the thatch of crisp, dry shrubbery.

Overhead two armed men walked to the edge of the canyon and peered down at the smoke and fire below, then turned back and disappeared.

Bolan quickly appraised his surroundings. The terrain between here and Nuevo Laredo typified the Mexico-Texas border. Periodically there would be a stretch of wooded area in which concealment and even cover from rifle fire would be no problem. But for the most part, he was facing a mixture of tangled dwarf trees and grasslands, trying to survive in what was otherwise open desert. The grasslands would provide little concealment once he left the ravine.

The desert would provide none at all.

The ravine appeared to be a semidry bed through which a river had once flowed. Bolan glanced over his shoulder. He needed to make it up the steep slope to the other side before pursuit started down. He had to put as much distance as possible between his empty Beretta and the assault rifle and machine pistol he'd just seen on the ridge.

Bolan moved quietly from cover and made his way up the red clay of the ravine wall. He was halfway to the top when the damp earth kicked into the air next to him. A split second later he heard the explosion of the assault rifle across the ravine.

More shots rang out as the warrior scrambled to the top and zigzagged toward a stand of trees in the distance. One round sliced the heel from his shoe as he ran, the force of the round knocking him forward. Bolan fell into a shoulder roll and was back on his feet, disappearing into the trees.

He stopped and peered back through the branches. The same two men had started down the embankment.

The Executioner took off across the rugged terrain. There was no way of telling how far the trees extended. Water was present below the surface of this semidesert country, but only sporadically did it rise close enough to the surface to support vegetation.

As he ran, he could see no break in the trees. He'd have cover for a while, but eventually the Executioner knew he'd be faced with more wide open prairie and desert.

He needed another battle plan. Fast.

Bolan ran as best he could, dodging limbs and making his way over rock and dehydrated shrubs. Slowing as he neared a dry creek bed, he heard his two pursuers crushing brittle twigs beneath their feet somewhere close behind.

As the warrior raced toward the creek bed, he found what he was looking for. A four-foot-long depression in the earth had eroded against the far bank. Stooping to where the water had once run, Bolan felt dry dirt on the surface. He dug down an inch with his fingers and came upon the same damp clay he'd encountered in the riverbed. Quickly he rubbed the red mud over his khaki slacks and brown pullover shirt, reaching down for more soil to cover his face and neck.

As the two men neared, the Executioner lifted a large branch from the ground and tossed it into the creek bed. Then he removed the heelless shoe from his foot and tossed it onto the other side of the creek bed before curling into the depression and pulling the branch over him.

The shoe would serve double duty—completely out of place in the wooded surroundings, it should catch the men's eyes the moment they neared the creek bed, diverting their attention from Bolan's hastily created camouflage. It should also lead them to believe that he'd lost the shoe as he sprinted through the trees, leading them past him.

Bolan watched through the twigs and dried leaves as the two men approached. The man with the machine pistol was about forty, his hair graying at the temples. As he neared, Bolan saw that the weapon was actually a barrel-shortened, French MAT submachine gun. His younger partner gripped a 5.56 mm SA 80 with a SUSAT sight mounted over the barrel. With its 4x magnification, the assault rifle could easily drop the Executioner on the open desert.

The two gunners halted as they approached the creek. "He won't get far now, Oswaldo," the younger man said in rapid Spanish. "Not in this country." He pointed over the creek bed at the shoe.

The older man frowned, scanning the area up and down the creek. "Don't be so sure. This man knows what he's doing. He might be hiding."

The other man laughed. "You're getting old, and you think like an old man. You're tired, so you think he must be also and has stopped to rest. No, this man has run on, and he has lost a shoe." The young man jumped over the creek bed.

"With age comes wisdom," Oswaldo replied. "I'll check here." He moved out of Bolan's field of vision and the Executioner heard more twigs crackle as the gunner searched the area.

Bolan waited almost fifteen minutes while the Mexican made his way from tree to tree before returning to poke along the creek bed with a sharpened stick. As he approached, the Executioner shifted his grip to the Beretta's barrel.

Oswaldo held the MAT with his right hand as he shoved the stick through the leaves over Bolan, its point stabbing into the earth mere inches from the Executioner's side.

Bolan grasped the end of the stick and held on, making it appear the sharp point was caught in mud.

The cartel man tugged gently, then jerked harder to loosen the probe.

Bolan rose like a ghost from the grave, letting the Mexican's man's own inertia assist him to his feet. He rapped the butt of the 93-R under the man's chin as he ascended.

Oswaldo's head snapped back as Bolan caught the barrel of the MAT and brought the Beretta around in an arc, crushing the gunner's windpipe. He wrenched the machine pistol away as the man fell to the ground, sputtering for air in his death throes.

The Executioner slung the MAT around his neck and bent forward, pulling an extra magazine from the back pocket of the corpse's pants. He found a large Buck folding knife on the man's belt, which he stuck into his waistband before moving on.

After crossing the creek, he pried the heel from his good shoe before stepping back into the one on the ground. He shifted his weight from side to side. His balance was better, but the heelless soles wouldn't last long over the rough terrain of northern Mexico.

Bolan followed broken limbs and occasional footprints in the dried leaves as he stalked the young gunner. He moved cautiously, fully aware that the kill range of the SA 80 far outdistanced the subgun in his hands.

He had to get inside the range of the assault rifle without being spotted first. Like a stocky prizefighter inside the reach of his longer-armed opponent, Bolan had to first pass through the danger zone to be effective.

Far ahead Bolan spotted a clearing through the trees. First he detected only movement, then, as he moved closer, a light blue color foreign to the surroundings came into focus.

The Executioner slowed his pace even more, careful to step over and around the dried debris in his path. Fifty yards from the clearing he dropped to the ground and crawled to cover behind a large rock at the edge of the trees.

The man in the blue work shirt sat astride a fallen tree. The SA 80 leaned against the trunk as he guided a gold coke spoon to his nose. Bolan let him fill both nostrils before he rose and walked into the clearing.

The Mexican dived for the assault rifle just as Bolan stitched a 9 mm pattern up his torso from belt to neck.

Walking cautiously forward, he knelt beside the body. The coke spoon was still gripped in the fingers of the man's right hand.

Bolan unlaced the brown work boots from the dead man's feet and slid into them. A little tight, but they'd get him back to Nuevo Laredo with nothing worse than blisters.

Hoisting the SA 80, he walked out of the clearing.

Bolan reached the outskirts of Nuevo Laredo by nightfall. He had carried both the MAT and SA 80 as he made his way back toward town, discarding them finally when the threat of being spotted by local citizens became of greater concern than the cartel.

He didn't need some frightened farmer calling the *federales*. Gringos with automatic weapons were not smiled upon by the Mexican authorities.

Bolan had kept to the bush as much as possible, paralleling Highway 85 until he'd been forced into the open again. Even then he had stayed as far from the road as he could.

Earlier in the day he'd recognized several vehicles belonging to cartel henchmen as they roared down the highway toward town. But as he neared the city lights, Bolan had seen no similar traffic for hours. When an ancient, rattling flatbed truck appeared on the horizon heading north, the Executioner rose to the road and flagged it down.

He still had to get through town, and a mud-covered American would attract less attention in the cab of a truck than he would walking in off the prairie.

The warrior rubbed what dirt he could from his face as the truck slowed to a halt. He swung himself up and into the cab, joining a gray-haired, mustachioed man, two chickens and a one-eyed dog. The truck had been old before Bolan was born; the man and dog seemed to predate it.

Long years of battle on every front had taught the soldier that when fortune presented an opportunity to rest, he must take advantage of it. He leaned back against the tattered seat and closed his eyes, listening to the grind of the gears as the truck choked its way toward the lights of the border town.

The old man chattered continuously in both Spanish and broken English, explaining that he transported bottled water from Monterrey to Nuevo Laredo once a week. Bolan learned detailed biographies on the dog and the chickens, and the old Mexican had just started in on his wife and six daughters when they slowed to a stop in the downtown market area.

Bolan handed the old man a thousand-peso note, seeing surprise register on the wrinkled face. "You haven't seen me," he said as he opened the truck door. "Okay?"

The wrinkles disappeared in joy and greed. "I haven't seen anyone."

ONCE BOLAN REACHED his murky room on the Vega Hotel's second floor, he checked to make sure the Desert Eagle and the rest of his gear was still hidden between the mattress and box springs. Satisfied, he reloaded the Beretta, then tossed his ragged, sweat-soaked clothes into the wastebasket before stepping into the shower.

Bolan was fastening the last button on a fresh shirt when he heard the muffled voices through the open window to the courtyard. Moving cautiously to peer through the partly open curtains, he looked down to see the odd assortment of Mexican police and cartel gunmen.

The Executioner watched as one of the gunners passed a fistful of pesos to the gray-haired old man from the water truck and then sent him on his way.

Bolan quietly slipped on the shoulder rig and cinched the Beretta into place. He had only a carryall of ammunition and one suitcase containing clothes. Zipping the small bag, he decided to donate the remainder of his clothing to any members of the hotel staff who could wear his size.

The warrior moved silently back to the corner of the window where the party below had just entered the hotel, leaving a lone uniformed policeman to guard the courtyard.

It was against the Executioner's code to do battle with law-enforcement officers of any country. However inefficient they might be, regardless of how tightly their hands were bound with the red tape of bureaucracy, he considered them allies in his lifelong war on crime.

Unless, like the old man from the water truck, they decided to play both ends against the middle.

Crooked cops were the lowest criminal life-form in the Executioner's opinion. They were twice guilty, having perverted and taken advantage of the public trust with which they'd been bestowed.

It appeared that the Mexican officials Bolan now heard climbing the stairs fit into this category, having struck some deal with the wealthy, powerful cartel.

But appearances could be deceiving. And just as with the masked men at the ranch, Bolan would take no chance of wrongfully killing honest men. The police he was about to face might just as easily be unknowing accomplices, victims of an elaborate cartel lie: an

American attacked and robbed the Rodriguez ranch. He killed Manuel Rodriguez and a dozen other men.

As he heard the arrival of the mixed party in the hallway outside the room, Bolan looked down to the shabby policeman in the courtyard. Uniform shirt unbuttoned in the heat, the man stood smoking a hand-rolled cigarette. He glanced occasionally upward but obviously felt no imminent threat from the window above.

That was his first mistake.

The second came when Bolan descended from the second-story window like a hawk swooping down on his prey. The surprised cop instinctively lowered his head against the attack, and the Executioner brought an elbow down on the back of his neck as he landed. The cigarette flew from the unconscious man's mouth as he fell forward, giving Bolan time to turn back to the window.

Ripping the Desert Eagle from his waistband, the Executioner fired four thunderous rounds from the .44, aiming high over the window. Adobe dust and splinters of wood fell harmlessly over an eight-point khaki hat that appeared momentarily in the opening, then ducked back inside.

By the time the police and cartel gunners descended the stairs, Bolan had covered the courtyard and was halfway down the alley that led to the marketplace.

He stopped abruptly at the end of the alley, tearing the shoulder rig from his back. He pulled off his shirt and replaced the holster on bare skin before concealing it under the shirt. The big .44 went into the carryall.

Bolan slowed his pace, walking casually down the bustling streets of the tourist area, past souvenir stands toward the parking garage where he'd left the rented

Buick. Slabs of curried goat hung in the windows of butcher shops along the way, their enticing scent reminding the soldier that he hadn't eaten since morning. Ignoring the hunger, he moved on.

The garage was locked at 9:00 p.m., and Bolan knew he'd have to devise a method of entry without attracting attention.

He never got the chance.

Two blocks from the parking garage, Bolan rounded the corner past a neon sign advertising The Millionaire of Burlesque, and walked straight into the barrel of a .45.

The small man behind the automatic held the gun with both hands and smiled, revealing a solid row of gold teeth that matched the multitude of chains at his throat. The Executioner quickly noted the diamond stud in the man's left ear and the diamond and gold on the fingers gripping the gun.

Cartel, all the way.

No Mexican cop, even on the take, could afford an array of jewelry like that.

Bolan swept the .45 to the side and shoved the carryall into the grinning gold teeth. The .45 exploded into the street as the Executioner brought his foot upward in an arc, catching the gunner squarely in the groin. The man's screams were lost in the carnivallike street noise as Bolan wrested the automatic from his grip, thrust it within point-blank range and fired.

The two gunshots drew police and cartel gunners like vultures to a carcass. Bolan ducked into the burlesque club as gunfire pounded the entrance around him. Holding the .45 close to his body he pushed his way through the crowd and smoke. On stage at the rear of the bar, four seminude, lewdly gyrating women belted out an off-key rendition of "The Banana Boat Song."

Over his shoulder Bolan saw two uniforms enter the doorway, guns drawn. Making his way slowly through the press of sweating bodies, he neared the stage and saw that the only other exit lay somewhere behind the curtain.

As Bolan reached the platform, a tall muscular bouncer in a skintight tank top stepped in front of him. In an obviously practiced movement, the muscle man raised a sawed-off baseball bat and swung smoothly at the Executioner's head.

Bolan ducked under the attack, stepped forward and brought the barrel of the .45 down across the bridge of the burly man's nose. Blood gushed from the shattered bone and cartilage as the thick body met the floor like a felled oak.

The Executioner vaulted the steps, hearing gunshots followed by screams behind him. At the rear of the stage he dived through the curtain, coming up in a dressing room. A dozen barely dressed women looked up in surprise as the Executioner rolled to his feet and sailed toward the back door.

Finding it locked, Bolan lowered his shoulder and hit the door, splintering rotten wood from the frame as he burst into the dimly lighted alley.

He was greeted by two more cartel gunners. Bolan fired twice into the first man, tagging him in the face and throat before diving behind a trash can.

The second gunner raised the twin barrels of a sawed-off shotgun, pulled both triggers and sent the scatter-load high over Bolan's head. Grasping under his sport coat, the man almost removed a revolver before the Executioner emptied the .45 into his chest.

Bolan dropped the useless weapon and pulled the Desert Eagle from the carryall. Sprinting down the alley, he tried the first door he came to and found it unlocked. As he closed it behind him he heard the rapid footfalls of his pursuers as they raced down the alley, cursing and arguing in Spanish.

Bolan found himself in an empty storage room that was stacked high with cases of whiskey, wine and beer. The store's proprietor looked up from his newspaper as the Executioner raced into view. Before the startled man could react, the warrior was through the front door and halfway down the street.

Gaining distance from the confusion, he slowed his pace and hid the .44 under his shirt as he blended in with the tourists in the marketplace.

A darkened side street took Bolan from the busy commerce area to a supermarket in the native section of town. He left the shadows for the crowded parking lot, dropping behind a car as a lone police vehicle sped by, siren screaming.

The second car he tried, a Lincoln Mark VII, was unlocked. He slid behind the wheel, ducking under the dash to join wires until the powerful engine coughed to life. Seeing no more signs of pursuit, he threw the car into reverse and backed onto the street.

Leaving the lights of Nuevo Laredo behind him, the Executioner drove southwest on Highway 2 toward Reynosa. It would be senseless to return to the ranch now. They would be ready and waiting.

But that state of heightened awareness wouldn't last forever. Soon, it would wear off and the cartel would feel secure in their operation once more.

Then the Executioner would return to carry on the fight.

Halfway between Camargo and Reynosa, Bolan cut the lights, left the highway and pulled onto an all but forgotten cow path that led to the river. The reflection of the moon off the Rio Grande was his only guide as he eased the Lincoln onto the rickety wooden bridge that connected two nations.

He'd take other back roads on the U.S. side of the border, coming out near McAllen, Texas, where he could abandon the Mark VII in some parking lot. An anonymous phone call to the local authorities would ensure its return to the rightful owner in Mexico.

And soon, another rightful return would be made. Bolan would rightfully return to a ranch just outside the border city of Nuevo Laredo.

The Executioner didn't believe in leaving a job half-done.

BOLAN THOUGHT of the motel bed that awaited him as he walked down the street from the Wal-Mart store to the Quo Vadis Inn. Stopping at a phone booth midway between the store and the motel, he dropped a quarter into the slot and dialed the McAllen police department. He gave the desk officer the Lincoln's description and location before hanging up when the man asked for his name. Wearily he circled the swimming pool to get to his room at the rear of the parking lot.

Bolan pulled the Beretta and Desert Eagle from his waistband and dropped them on the bed, then unzipped the carryall and removed a gun cleaning kit.

Brognola had been out of the office when he'd called earlier, and it was vital that he talk to the man from Justice before he proceeded. Bolan glanced at the pillows on the bed as he sat down. There was no point in trying to sleep until the return call came. He ejected the magazine from the Beretta and worked the slide, jacking the chambered round onto the bed next to him. Then, flipping the slide release, he dismantled the weapon.

There had been rumors for the past couple of years of a mysterious group of mercenaries operating along the Mexican-American border. They specialized in recovering airplanes that had been stolen in the U.S. and were then used to smuggle drugs from Mexico back across the border. The Mexicans, ever ready to romanticize their enemies, had named them the Vampire Bats. Bolan remembered the odd black Kevlar vests and hoods. The more he thought about it, the more ready he was to believe that this was the group who had attacked the ranch and taken the Cessna. But he had to make sure.

Twisting the cap from a bottle of solvent, he threaded a small cloth patch through the eye of the cleaning rod. He had just dipped it into the bottle when the phone rang. He picked up the receiver.

"Striker." Brognola sounded tired.

Bolan held the receiver in place with his ear and shoulder, running the cleaning rod up and down the Beretta's barrel as he spoke. "I need some quick intel, Hal," he said, ignoring formalities. "There's a group of mercenaries operating along the border—"

Brognola chuckled. "For once I'm a step ahead of you, guy. I got a call about three this morning from an old acquaintance who's evidently the ringmaster of that circus."

"I noticed you said 'acquaintance.' "

"You got it. Guy's name is Buddy Taylor. Think back. Ring a bell?"

"Yeah. Vaguely." Bolan set the barrel on the bed as his mind raced back over the years to the time and place where he'd first seen combat. "Buddy Taylor. War hero...for a while. There were rumors of black market dealings, the needless slaughter of civilians."

"Right," Brognola said. "He was stationed for a while at Kaeson. My guess is that the rumors were true, or at least based on fact. He got caught with his hand in the cookie jar again in Vietnam. Seems there wasn't enough evidence for a court martial, but they pressured him out with a general discharge."

Bolan pressed a rag against the mouth of the solvent bottle and turned it upside down, letting the cloth absorb a small amount of the liquid. He picked up the Beretta's frame and began rubbing it down. "You've done your homework. But why'd he call you?"

"Seems that this time he's taken a bigger bite of the action than he was prepared to chew. Taylor's avoided cartel operations up until now, but he made a mistake this time. A big mistake. Not only was this a Colombian op, the Cessna they flew out was already loaded with coke."

"How much is he sitting on?" Bolan asked.

"Over three hundred keys. That's not the biggest shipment they've ever run, but it's enough to severely irritate the cartel drug lords. I guess the plane was so loaded down they couldn't even get it all in the hidden compartments they'd built. It was under the seats, on the floor. Everywhere." Brognola paused. "If it hadn't been, he might not ever have found it. Anyway, it's already cost Taylor two men. By the way, Striker, he mentioned some mysterious American who was shooting dopers at the ranch yesterday."

"You said he lost two men, Hal. I only saw one go down."

"Well, the one you saw lived long enough to give up the identities of the rest. One of his pilots caught a couple of .22s in the brain when he got home. The cartel justice department works considerably faster than mine."

Bolan frowned. "How does he know the hit was cartel? Guys like him make a lot of enemies."

"According to the cops who investigated, the pilot's name was Randall Axe. The report says he was found with his throat slit and the tongue pulled down and out through the gash. Sound familiar?"

Bolan felt his fingers tighten around the gun frame. "Colombian necktie."

"Right. Anyway, Mr. Taylor is scared to death, and he proposed a trade. He'll give us the cocaine in exchange for a new face under the Witness Protection Program."

"You didn't go for it, did you?"

"Well," Brognola said, "yes and no. I agreed...with one stipulation. Taylor's got to finger all cartel operations and any other drug locations he knows about."

"And?"

"And he's not crazy about the idea. He's worried about testifying in court."

"Considering who we're dealing with, I'd say that's a pretty legitimate concern on his part."

"Yes, it is. But I told him not to worry. I was fairly sure that the man I sent with him would make sure things never got to court." Brognola paused. "You interested?"

Bolan set the gun frame on the bed. "I haven't hung up, have I? I'm going back to finish things at the ranch, one way or another. I can follow whatever trail I find there and eventually locate the other cartel sites, but this would be faster. Tell me about the rest of Taylor's group."

Bolan began rubbing a light coat of oil over the parts of the Beretta. He could hear the rustling of papers on the other end of the line before Brognola answered. "He uses a variety of people, but he's got three regulars," the Justice man said. "Guy named Jackson. Nothing spectacular on him. Regular Army for seven years before he busted out on drug charges. Then there's a woman, Janie Brewer. I don't know if you'll want her in on the deal or not."

"We'll see how it goes. Who's the third member of the team?"

"He's the interesting one. A Cuban name Felipe Valdez, formerly with Alpha 66."

Bolan frowned. Alpha 66 was a CIA-sponsored unit of Cuban nationals that operated out of the Florida Keys, running frequent guerrilla attacks against the Castro regime. The expatriate Cubans were zealots in their quest to rid their homeland of communism. So what was Valdez doing working for a bush-league merc like Buddy Taylor?

Brognola read his mind. "Seems that Valdez was in charge of funds for his unit and his fingers got a little sticky. The Cubans let him go."

"He's lucky they let him live."

"Yeah. It seems there were extenuating circumstances that influenced them. Something about using the money to help his sister get out of Cuba. It's not real clear."

Bolan dropped the cleaning rag and began reassembling the 93-R. "Anything else I need to know?" he asked Brognola.

"Yeah. One other thing. I'm out on a limb on this one. Taylor insisted on holding the cocaine until after it's all over. I don't like it, but I was afraid if I pushed too hard he might decide he had a better chance of survival by trying to return the dope to the Colombians."

"They'd kill him anyway."

Brognola sighed. "I know that, and you know that. But I'm not sure *he* does. The only reason he's willing to trade with us at all is the fact that he doesn't know how to sell the coke himself without attracting a lot of attention."

"Honorable man I'll be working with."

"Right."

Bolan stifled a yawn. "You set up a meeting?" He shoved the magazine up the well of the Beretta and worked the slide, chambering a round while Brognola gave him the time and place.

"Anything else you'll need right now?" the big Fed asked.

The warrior thought for a moment, then said, "Yeah. Get in touch with Grimaldi. Tell him to pick a fast bird and stand by."

Bolan returned the phone to its cradle. He was determined to take his war all the way to the top of the Medellín cartel, which would eventually entail a trip to Colombia. When, exactly, he couldn't be sure of, and Grimaldi would have to be ready for takeoff at a moment's notice.

Bolan rose from the bed and walked into the bathroom. He twisted the tap in the sink, leaned down and splashed cold water onto his face. Looking up into the mirror, he stared at the dark circles beneath his eyes.

He had to sleep sometime, and if the opportunity ever presented itself, Bolan decided he would.

3

The light bulb in the *L* of the Starlight Inn's neon sign flickered twice, then died as Bolan pulled the rented Corvette into the parking lot. He cut the engine, removed the keys and opened the door, feeling the torrid heat of the southern Arizona evening hit his face like a left hook.

The inn lay, dying a slow death, on the northern edge of Yuma, Arizona. The odor of strong, heavily seasoned cooking wafted steadily through the open door as Bolan crossed the gravel lot to room 113.

He had mixed emotions as he raised a fist to knock. It would have been foolish to slowly track down the cartel installations in Mexico from the scant evidence he knew he'd find at the ranch. Sure, he'd eventually find the links needed to close the gap between the Rodriguez ranch and the kingpins in Colombia. He didn't need a broken-down, slovenly mercenary to make the connection. But Buddy Taylor could have time, valuable time that could then be spent in countless other areas of Bolan's continuing war. And the Vampire Bat commander had firsthand knowledge of the strike zones. That knowledge could prove invaluable in planning each attack.

If Taylor could be trusted.

The Executioner had been on the cutting edge long enough to know that an informant's motivation rarely came from the goodness in his heart. Good "snitches" weren't recruited from the rolls of Sunday school classes. An informant who had never been dirty himself rarely had the inside knowledge necessary to be of value.

They were a necessary evil, Bolan supposed, but he'd never get used to the idea of teaming up with men like Buddy Taylor—small-time mercenaries, semiskilled, semiorganized, semitrustworthy.

Bolan recalled their abduction of the Cessna. They had been only too ready to desert one another in the heat of battle. The Beechcraft's pilot had flown off without Taylor, and Taylor had not only deserted his fallen comrade but attempted to protect his own identity by firing at the wounded man.

Facts to remember, Bolan told himself, as he heard the lock thrown back inside the room. He was surprised when the door opened to reveal a tall, striking woman in her mid-twenties. Her canary yellow hair cascaded in layered ringlets past shoulders left bare by a cherry-red tube top. Bolan briefly noted the bare midriff before his battle senses went on alert.

It was all too obvious what was about to happen.

Smiling sexily, the woman inched the door wider. "Come on in, sugar. Been waiting for you . . . *so long*."

Bolan almost yawned. He could have written the script for the scene he knew would follow. Stepping through the doorway into the obvious trap, he waited patiently until he felt the cold steel of a gun barrel make contact with his left temple.

"Don't even breathe," said a raspy smoker's voice from behind the door.

The Executioner brought his left arm up and over in an arc, sweeping the gun from his head in one smooth movement. Turning to face the voice, he grabbed the short barrel of a .357 and twisted it away from his body. He heard a surprised shriek as the man's index finger caught in the trigger guard. Changing the angle of twist slightly, he spared the gunman a broken finger and pulled the revolver neatly from his grasp. Bolan encircled the other man's neck in a headlock and jammed the barrel of the gun tightly against the balding scalp.

The bathroom door flew open and two men armed with shotguns burst into the room, grinning. The grins faded as they ground to a halt, confronting a reversal of the scene they'd expected.

"Drop the scatterguns in the corner," Bolan commanded. The two men, one Caucasian and the other Hispanic, carefully leaned their shotguns against the wall next to the desk.

"Now, any other weapons," Bolan said.

The short, stocky Hispanic dropped a Browning Hi-Power and a stag-handled Bowie knife next to the shotguns. The Caucasian's sparse, unruly mustache drooped as he added a Government Model .45, a Colt Mustang .38 and a Gerber Guardian boot knife to the pile.

Bolan shook his head. "You boys and your toys." He motioned them toward the far wall of the room, then pressed the revolver into his prisoner's spine as he shook the man down, finding only an Al Mar SERE combat blade in a pouch on his belt.

"What? No grenades?" Bolan asked, then shoved the man across the room toward his comrades. He glanced quickly at the tight clothing on the woman, determined it provided little opportunity for concealment, then met her eyes. She returned his look with a smile of surprise and admiration.

Bolan walked to the corner where the weapons were piled and tossed the snubbie .357 into the heap. Drawing the Desert Eagle, he turned the desk chair around and sat down, arms hanging over the backrest. The massive .44 dangled casually from his right hand. "One of you combat experts is Taylor, I assume?"

The paunchy man he'd held prisoner stepped forward, red-faced and breathing hard. "Me," he growled.

"Good. Let's get a few things straight up front. First, I get the definite impression that this little drama you orchestrated was to make it clear who's in charge. Well, it did." He waited for a reply. When no one spoke, he continued. "Second, I get the feeling that you're not crazy about working with me."

"You got that right, Pollock," Taylor said, using the cover name Bolan had selected for this mission.

"That's fine, too," Bolan answered. "I'm not thrilled with the situation, either. As far as I'm concerned, you're not a half length higher on the food chain than the scum you steal planes from. You're sitting on a load of coke that you'd have already turned if you were smart enough to know how. That makes you two things in my book—criminal and stupid. Your performances just now confirmed the stupid part."

Taylor grunted and took a half step forward, then changed his mind, his eyes falling to the huge weapon filling the Executioner's hand.

Bolan smiled and returned the Desert Eagle to the holster beneath his coat. "Okay. Now that we're clear on the chain of command and our feelings about each other, let's get down to business. You can pick up your toys now."

Slowly and unsurely, like schoolboys in the principal's office, the three men retrieved the various weapons and took seats around the room. Taylor introduced both Gus Jackson and Felipe Valdez. None of the men shook hands.

Bolan looked at the woman reclining seductively on the bed.

"This is Janie Brewer," Taylor told him. "Part-time singer, part-time model."

Janie smiled coyly at Bolan, uncrossing her legs and raising one knee slightly.

"And full-time whore," Taylor finished, oblivious to the look Janie shot his way. "She turns tricks when she's broke, and she works with me when I need a woman." Taylor laughed boorishly. "In more ways than one."

"In your dreams, old man," Janie scoffed. She turned to Bolan. "I'm a damn good actress. Both on and off stage. But I'm broke most of the time. If you need me for anything—" Janie's tongue licked her lower lip, leaving a shiny wet glow "—I'm available."

Bolan ignored her and turned back to the men. "We begin tomorrow morning. I want to strike hard and fast. To put it simply, we hit every drug compound you're familiar with, then follow whatever trails we find back to Colombia. There's bound to be big names on the other end. I don't know what those names are yet, but I will by the time we're through in Mexico."

"Hey, wait a minute," Taylor said. "Our deal was to *show* you where to go. Not go with you."

"That's fine, Taylor. To tell you the truth, I'd prefer it that way myself. I don't need a lot of drugstore soldiers weighing me down when it hits the fan. But unfortunately you'll have to be there. I won't have time to drop you off at the local cantina after you've fingered the strike zones. Whether you fire a shot or not is up to you. But stay the hell out of my way."

Bolan turned to Valdez. "All intelligence indicates that the prime cartel distribution point is on the Baja Peninsula, probably near La Paz. You're Cuban, right?"

"*Sí*. A patriot."

Bolan raised his eyebrows in surprise. The man's accent was that of northern Mexico. While they might speak a common language, the difference in Cuban and Mexican pronunciation was as marked as that of a London cockney and an Alabama farm boy. "What's your training background?" he asked Valdez.

"Recon. Infiltration and communications," the Cuban said proudly. Straightening in his chair, he added, "I was with Alpha 66."

Bolan nodded. Valdez's association with Alpha 66 explained the Mexican accent. Linguists, provided by the CIA, would have removed all traces of Cuban pronunciation with hours of grueling speech lessons.

He remembered what Brognola had told him about Valdez's dismissal from Alpha and wondered again if this might be just a good man gone wrong.

"Can you pass as a Mexican?" Bolan asked the Cuban.

"Easily." Valdez smiled. "I have done so many times."

"Good. Because you're on your way to La Paz."

The Cuban nodded.

Bolan rose from the chair and crossed the room to the door. Then, turning back to the woman on the bed, he said, "Have you eaten yet?"

"Eaten *who*?" Taylor snickered.

Janie shot him a dirty look, then returned her eyes to Bolan. A surprised expression replaced her anger. "No," she said, standing up. "I haven't."

Bolan opened the door and waited while she crossed the room, oblivious to the obscene leers of Taylor and Jackson.

"Hell, at least the son of a bitch is human," he heard Taylor drawl as he closed the door behind them.

THE WAGON WHEEL CAFÉ was located across the gravel parking lot of the Starlight Inn. A chalkboard in the grease-stained window claimed it had remained open round-the-clock for the past thirty-two years, four months and six days.

Bolan's steak tasted like it had been broiled during the Wagon Wheel's grand opening and rewarmed after the waitress took his order.

He pushed the leatherlike strip to the side and chewed on a french fry while he studied the hand-scrawled cardboard signs on the wall. They announced, in misspelled words, both the daily specials and the fact that service would be refused to anyone not wearing shoes and a shirt. In the booth behind Janie Brewer, two unshaven men in baseball caps argued sex, ranching and politics in no particular order of importance. On the far side of the room, a young deputy sheriff divided his attention between a bowl of chili and sporadic attempts to catch Janie's eyes.

Bolan watched silently as Janie picked at her taco salad. She had become more subdued since his dinner invitation but seemed to be enjoying herself. He poured coffee into both cups from the plastic pot on the table. Janie smiled up in surprise.

It was all too obvious how the world had broken this woman. Like a mongrel dog, kicked and beaten by its master, she was now willing to lick the hand of anyone showing her even the smallest semblance of kindness.

Janie gave up on the salad and dabbed her lips with a napkin. "Thank you," she said.

Bolan smiled. "Not exactly the Ritz, is it?"

"I don't mean for the food. You're right. It's pretty awful. I mean . . . thank you for bringing me here. Getting me out of there for a while."

Bolan nodded. "I'm not usually a big one for clichés," he said. "But under the circumstances, this one seems unavoidable."

Janie laughed. "'What's a nice girl like me' and all that?"

"Exactly."

"I'm a performer." Janie shrugged. "I'm good. But it takes more than talent. You've got to have luck, too. And so far, I haven't. I guess I've never been in the right place at the right time." Janie's eyes fell to her plate as her cheeks reddened. "And a girl has to eat somehow."

"How'd you meet Taylor?" Bolan asked.

She paused, then lifted her eyes to meet his. "Well, I was dating a guy who worked for him. Nice guy. I wasn't in love or anything, but he treated me well."

"Jackson?" Bolan wondered. Somehow it didn't seem to fit.

"No, Lord no," Janie said, laughing quickly. "I've never been *that* hungry. It was another guy." She raised her water glass to her lips, then returned it to the table. "He got shot in one of the early missions. Right out of the sky, I guess. It was when they used to parachute in."

Bolan frowned. "That doesn't explain your involvement."

Janie fumbled briefly with the cellophane on a package of crackers before setting it down. "It's not always airplanes, you know. Taylor got a different kind of job shortly after my boyfriend got killed. He'd recovered a plane for this guy earlier, I guess. Well, the guy was married to a Mexican woman. She took off with their baby and went back home. No legal way he could get his son back, so he hired Taylor again."

Janie stopped as the waitress reappeared to fill their water glasses. When the woman left, she continued. "Taylor hired me to go along and take care of the baby on the way back. I was between jobs . . . so I went."

Bolan stared at the woman across the table. The story had holes in it from top to bottom. He said nothing.

Janie picked the crackers up again and nervously struggled for the opening before slamming them back to the table. "Okay, dammit. I was hooking. I was tired of working, slinging hash in hellholes like this one and waiting to hit the big time. There wasn't any boyfriend, and there wasn't any baby. Taylor was one of my tricks. That's how I met him."

Bolan remained silent. He had guessed that Taylor's accusations concerning Janie's prostitution were accurate, and he hadn't believed the unlikely story about the baby. But it had not been until Janie actually admitted the lie and her true meeting with Taylor that the Executioner had drawn the painful parallel that now tore at his soul.

Bolan's mind drifted back over the years to the events that had spawned his lifelong quest to eradicate evil, to another innocent girl, younger than Janie, who'd been forced onto the deadly, one-way road of prostitution.

Forced not by the dream of stardom, but by a more immediate threat: the Mafia.

Bolan's sister had sold herself in an attempt to save their father from the wrath of the Mob. It hadn't worked.

A soft tap on his clenched fist brought Bolan back to the present.

"Hey, you in there?" Janic asked.

Bolan returned his attention to the woman across from him. "Sorry," he told her. "My mind drifted for a minute."

"I told you I was a good actress. You almost bought the part about the baby, didn't you?"

Bolan smiled. "Almost."

Janie giggled, an innocent, girlish brightness transforming her face. It was suddenly replaced by a pleading expression. "I'm not really one of them," she said softly. "Not really."

Bolan studied her face as she returned her attention to the salad, poking uneasily with her fork. "Tell me about Valdez," he said.

"He's different, too. I know he worked for that Cuban bunch in Florida or somewhere. Against Castro, I think. He's nicer than the others. Sad, though. The other Cubans kicked him out."

Bolan frowned. "He tell you all that?"

Janie shrugged her shoulders and stared guiltily back at her plate. "We . . . became close for a while. He got drunk one night and cried and told me the whole story. He just wanted to get his sister out of Cuba. He was ashamed. She'd been forced to become the mistress of somebody high up in the government. He never said who. That's what the money was for. He wasn't going to keep it or anything."

Bolan nodded. "Did she escape?"

Janie shook her head. "No. Something happened. Felipe never said what. I don't know...I guess she's still in Cuba." Janie paused. "Taylor doesn't trust him."

"Why's that?"

"I overheard him talking to Jackson, once. Valdez is still dedicated to the cause. He's dedicated to something other than money. That's bound to be something Buddy can't understand, right there. I guess the old man's afraid Valdez's principles might get in the way someday."

The waitress shuffled over. "Get you anything else?" she asked.

Bolan saw Janie glanced from his cardboard steak to her uneaten salad before answering. "No, thanks," she said. "My system's taken enough chances for one night."

The waitress shrugged, slapped a grease-splattered check upside down on the table and staggered away.

Bolan set her tip by the unfinished steak and they rose to leave.

"What about Jackson?" he asked as they crossed the lot back to the Starlight Inn.

Janie stiffened. "Sort of a Buddy Taylor clone. Not as smart, but just as mean." She stopped, grasping Bolan's arm before self-consciously dropping it again. Looking up into the big man's eyes, she added, "I wouldn't trust either one of them. Not if I were you."

Bolan escorted Janie up the stairs to her room on the Starlight's second floor. She fished through her purse, came up with the key and inserted it into the lock. She turned to face Bolan once again. "Would you...like to come in?" she asked. The flush of red he'd seen earlier rushed to her cheeks. "For a drink or something...I mean...for a drink?"

"Thanks," Bolan said, "but I've got a lot of things to do before tomorrow."

Janie bit her bottom lip and nodded. "We could... just talk some more."

Bolan shook his head. "I'm sorry," he told her.

Janie smiled sadly, said good-night and closed the door.

THE PEDESTRIAN LINE at the border was long but moving steadily as Bolan fell in at the end. Directly ahead of him, two Oriental men in gaudy print beach shirts snapped photographs as they meandered along, indiscriminately recording everything they saw. Instinctively Bolan turned sideways and rubbed both eyes to conceal his face as their cameras turned randomly on him.

Jackson had crossed earlier that morning. Bolan and Taylor had watched him through binoculars from a third-story motel room two blocks away. It had gone smoothly and without incident. That, combined with the speed with which the line was moving, reassured the Executioner that there was no serious search being conducted at the crossing.

There rarely was. Contraband and illegal aliens travelled north across the Rio Grande, not south.

Bolan resisted the impulse to pat the spots where the Desert Eagle and Beretta were concealed. The overcast sky had provided him with the excuse he needed for a light raincoat and enabled him to hide both weapons and their appropriate harnesses.

The lone U.S. customs officer cupped his hands against the breeze and lighted a cigarette as the Executioner passed unnoticed into Mexico.

Returning to Nuevo Laredo's market area, he walked quickly through the shops and tourists to the café where Jackson should be waiting. Buddy Taylor would cross the border in half an hour and join them. After the initial strike on the Rodriguez ranch, Bolan would take the show on the road, expanding his never-ending war to include other drug compounds pointed out by Taylor.

He thought back in disgust to Taylor's disheveled appearance that morning. While crossing into Mexico armed with illegal weapons should pose no problem, the customs men weren't fools. Taylor's seedy image was bound to draw attention. Bolan had finally ordered him to shower, shave and wear a clean shirt.

Spotting the café, he walked through the door to find Jackson seated at a splintered wooden table, a shot of tequila in front of him, and a woman on each side. The Executioner approached the table as Jackson tucked a dollar bill down the neckline of one of the them. The spotty hairs in his mustache spread and curled over his top lip as he leaned forward, whispering into the woman's ear. Whatever he said sent her into a fit of laughter.

Bolan motioned for the women to leave. They glanced quickly at Jackson, who shrugged indifferently. Looking back to Bolan, their expressions changed and they quickly crossed the room and sat at a table against the wall.

The warrior took the seat across from Jackson and reached for the shot glass. He slowly poured the clear liquid onto the dry clay floor. "We've got work to do," he said.

Jackson shrugged his shoulders again. "Suits me. The old man on his way?"

"Thirty minutes."

"Then what?"

"We go pick up the car I left here last week," Bolan replied. "I've got weapons and other gear stashed in the trunk."

Jackson raised his heavy eyebrows. "You what?"

A waitress spotted the newcomer and walked to the table, interrupting the conversation. Bolan ordered coffee for both men. When the woman had left, Jackson continued. "You left a car here a week ago? You got to be kidding. There ain't gonna be nothin' left but the frame, if that."

The waitress returned and set two mugs onto the table. Bolan took a sip of the room-temperature brew.

The car would be fine. It was locked inside one of the city's most reputable parking garages. Bolan had known he might need it at a moment's notice and, uncertain how long he'd be tied up at the ranch, had paid the attendant two weeks' rent in advance. That, and the healthy tip he slipped the man, would ensure its safety.

But the Executioner felt neither the desire nor obligation to explain these details to the young man opposite him.

Bolan set down his mug and thought of Valdez. The little Cuban had called that morning to report. The false passport and matching ID the CIA had issued him years ago had enabled him to gain employment at the La Flora Lodge. La Flora was an exclusive resort near La Paz that doubled as the cover for the cartel's North American headquarters. Valdez was the new captain of the resort's fishing boat. But it was the second piece of intelligence Valdez had uncovered that caught the Executioner's interest.

The little Cuban had taken a man wahoo fishing that very morning. The man had been treated with the utmost respect, even by the resort manager.

The man's name was General Juan Montoya, and he was the commander-in-chief of Colombia's armed forces.

Valdez had proved himself to be more than adequate as an infiltrator. He had the ability to watch and observe, absorb all the details, then separate the wheat from the chaff.

There had been no doubt in his mind.

The leader of Colombia's armed forces was also the top man in the cartel.

Valdez had called back to update his report shortly before Bolan had crossed the border. Montoya was returning to Bogotá the next day.

Good, Bolan thought. By the time he got home, Janie Brewer would be in place.

The would-be actress was about to play an invaluable role in the operation. Valdez had noted that each night, Montoya chose a woman from the cartel resort's vast stable of prostitutes. Though the women varied, they were always tall, redheaded Americans.

Janie Brewer had been tall, American and blond when Bolan met her. She was now tall, American, red-haired and on a plane to Bogotá.

Bolan glanced across the room to the table against the wall. The women who'd been sitting with Jackson quickly looked away. The Executioner took another sip of the bitter coffee. He'd found Janie's early attempts to seduce him about as sexy as a bag of dirty laundry. But when she'd finally dropped the third-rate Lauren

Bacall impersonation, the wounded, insecure little girl in her had emerged. Bolan couldn't help but pity her. She was just another type of victim.

But she was smart. She'd be as adept at gathering the necessary information as Valdez. Maybe better.

The café door swung open, and Buddy Taylor swaggered through like the gunfighter in a low-budget Western. Bolan just shook his head. The situation would be comical if it wasn't so serious, but it was serious. It was literally a matter of life and death, and the warrior reminded himself that the cartel might not be his only enemy on this mission.

Taylor was an opportunist, at best. He'd already proved his willingness to play both ends against the middle. Add that to the fact that the Executioner had humiliated the aging mercenary in front of his men, and the man might be capable of anything in an attempt to regain face.

Bolan made a mental note to watch his back as well as his front. Without speaking, he rose and walked out to the dusty streets of Nuevo Laredo. Both men followed.

4

Buddy Taylor was beginning to wish he'd just taken his chances with the cartel. He was sick and tired of this whole mess—tired of being ordered around by Rance Pollock, and sick of the feeling he got in his belly when he thought of where they were going and what they were about to do. It just didn't make sense. He was about to risk his life for nothing.

They wouldn't make a penny by going back to the Rodriguez ranch.

Taylor glanced briefly at Pollock behind the wheel of the Buick, then stared out the window at the dark clouds taking shape overhead in the distance. It wasn't like he wasn't willing to risk his life. He'd done it before. But there had always been something in it for him when he did. Besides, it was one thing to fly in, grab a plane and get the hell out again. Half the time it was over before the beaners even figured out what was happening. The only rounds fired were the ones the Vampire Bats laid down themselves to add to the confusion.

It was another matter altogether to intentionally launch an attack against well-armed men. There were hundreds of thousands of dollars in dope at stake, and these cartel bastards were intent on protecting it. And they'd still be on guard after last week.

Taylor glanced again at the big man driving the car. What the hell was it all for? Honor? Justice? The American Way? Or did Pollock have some other silly-ass Boy Scout reason for helping Brognola?

No. It was all for nothing.

Taylor turned in the Buick's passenger seat and caught a glimpse of Jackson behind him. Stupid son of a bitch was playing with the .45 Pollock had given him. The gaping hole of the barrel was pointed directly at Taylor through the thin seat between them.

"You ever seen a .45 before?" he asked Jackson.

Jackson's head shot up. "Huh?"

"I asked if you've ever seen a gun like that before."

Wispy mustache hairs fell over Jackson's lips as he frowned. "Sure, Buddy. Plenty of times. You know that."

"Have you checked to make sure it's loaded?"

"Sure I did. Seven in the mag, one up the pipe."

"Then put the damn thing up before you blow a hole in me, Pollock or the car. You're fondling it like it was a woman."

The mustache sagged as Jackson returned the automatic to his side and sat sulking like a little boy reprimanded by his father. Then his eyes caught sight of the M-16 on the seat beside him. The smile returned as he lifted the weapon and cradled it in his arms.

Taylor shook his head in disgust and turned his back to the man as light drops of rain began to hit the hood of the Buick. Asshole. They were all assholes. From the semi-literate Neanderthal in the back seat to that crazy, Cuban flag-waver, Valdez.

Not to mention the bitch.

Buddy Taylor knew that Janie had never been his exclusive property. That was fine. He wouldn't have wanted it any other way. But she had always been there when he wanted her, needed her. For a price, of course, but available and convenient.

Then this bastard Pollock had shown up and taken over everything, and now the whore's legs were sealed tighter than his grandmother's canning jars. Taylor cast another quick glance at the big man behind the wheel of the Buick. One more reason to hate the son of a bitch.

Taylor closed his eyes and listened to the rain beat its metallic rhythm against the car roof. Well, it would be over soon. If he played his cards right, he'd be rid of them all. And as far as Janie went, there were other whores, whores who didn't kid themselves into thinking they were something they weren't.

And what they were about to do wasn't really for nothing, after all. Good old Witness Protection. He was getting a new face, a new life out of the deal. Not a bad swap.

If he lived to take advantage of it.

Taylor watched as Pollock twisted the knob, increasing the windshield wiper speed to accommodate the downpour. He studied the man in the tight black combat suit from the corner of his eye. Part of the aging merc was sure the guy was nuts, another psycho vigilante out to save a world that deserved what it got. But another part of Buddy Taylor grudgingly admitted he admired Rance Pollock. In many ways the man seemed to be everything Taylor had wanted to be since childhood—big, strong, fast, smart and sure of himself and what he was doing.

For a short period of time, years ago and continents away in Korea, Taylor had seen a piece of those qualities in himself. He had been a twenty-year-old soldier, secure in his beliefs and the war he was fighting. A warrior, untainted as yet by the lust for money and the almost sexual thrill he experienced from easy kills.

He had fought, not for his own profit or pleasure, but for the justness of his cause.

The merc pushed the uncomfortable thoughts from his mind and lighted a Camel. That was a long time ago. Before he grew up. Before he wised up. There *were* no causes worth dying for.

And the only cause he'd fight for was his own.

Pollock's voice roused him from his thoughts. "Fasten your seat belts." They turned down the muddy road that led to the ranch house.

Taylor snapped the buckle. "Crazy bastard," he muttered under his breath. Pollock was going to get him killed if he wasn't careful. If not here today, then later during some other hit.

The aging mercenary felt the weight of the M-16 in his lap. He had extra magazines and a Government Model .45 in the web belt on his hip. This lily-white knight had armed them well, even if he would have preferred his Thompson.

But this was okay. Taylor grinned to himself as the vehicle sloshed through the mud to the ranch house. These weapons would work just fine for what he had in mind—self-preservation. Find a nice, cozy, easily defended little corner somewhere and allow himself to be conveniently pinned down. Pollock could risk his ass if he wanted to. James Raymond Taylor would look out for numero uno.

He looked at the man behind the steering wheel as lightning flashed. Regardless of what happened in the next few minutes, this would be his one and only mission with this self-appointed avenging angel.

And Buddy Taylor was determined to survive it.

He was just as determined to make sure Rance Pollock didn't.

JANIE BREWER SPUN slowly on the bar stool and faced the empty stage of the Paradise Lounge. She chewed thoughtfully on a piece of ice from the glass in her hand. From somewhere in the back of her mind, she remembered that chewing ice was sometimes a symptom of sexual frustration, and wondered where that little fragment of knowledge had attached itself to her. Freshman psychology, probably.

The bartender looked up from the sink, water and soapsuds dripping from his hands. "Another Scotch?" he asked.

"No thanks. I go on right after we open. Gotta sound my best. First night and all . . ." Her voice trailed back into thought.

What would her life be like now if she'd stayed in college? Janie wondered. Would she still be chasing this same elusive dream of stardom? Probably. But with a degree in music or drama, she'd have teaching to fall back on when times were lean. She wouldn't be hooking, that was sure. She certainly wouldn't have gotten involved with Buddy Taylor and his crew of violent misfits.

And on those rare occasions when she met a man who attracted her, like Rance Pollock, she wouldn't have to be ashamed of the life she'd led.

Janie stared past the bartender, unseeing, as he moved throughout the room, pulling upturned chairs from the tabletops and positioning them on the floor. She felt a nervous flutter in her stomach; a pink flush colored her cheeks.

Damn. It was like being a schoolgirl again. It had been years since any man had affected her like this.

Rance had seemed totally immune to her flirtations—the same little tricks that sent most men leaping through hoops. Not only immune, he had appeared to be unaware of her very presence. In frustration she had given up the game, and suddenly he became friendly. Warm. Not interested in her body, but interested in her as a living, breathing human being, a person with hopes, dreams, strengths and weaknesses.

Rance Pollock was everything she believed a man should be. He was almost too good to be true.

And definitely too good for her. Men like that were few and far between. They were at a premium. They didn't have to settle for... whores. Janie walked behind the bar and filled her glass with ice water. She returned to the stool, wishing she'd stayed in college.

She felt the shame flow through her body. It would be nice if the circumstances were different. He'd be an easy man to fall for.

Janie Brewer got up and sauntered to the dressing room backstage and began the finishing touches before the first show. She looked critically into the mirror as she applied the bright red lipstick, focusing on the tiny wrinkles beginning to form at the corners of her mouth and eyes. They weren't too bad. Not yet. She still had a few good years in which to reach the top.

The thought brightened her spirits. Determination began to cut through the depression. Who knew? She might even make the right connections here in Bogotá. And there was always a slight chance that Rance felt the same for her that she did for him. Maybe he wouldn't care about her past. He seemed as secure and confident as anyone she'd ever met. Maybe it wouldn't intimidate him that she'd been a prostitute.

Through the thin wall, Janie heard the muffled chatter of the early arrivals. The band broke into its first set of dance numbers, typical south-of-the-border arrangements of American rock and 1940s swing, both managing to sound the same with the undermining Latin rhythm.

Then the manager was announcing her, and she was onstage, bending to pull the mike from its stand and making sure her deep cleavage was displayed to full advantage. Strolling to center stage, Janie propped one leg high on a stool, letting the slash in her red sequined gown fall open to reveal the top of her stocking and the garter that held it.

As she sang the first few words of her opening number, Janie spotted the man seated at the center table nearest the stage. He was surrounded by husky, rough-looking men who had to be bodyguards.

So he *had* come.

He was the reason she had picked the Paradise over the many other clubs and lounges in Bogotá. It was favored above all by General Juan Montoya.

Janie stared directly into the general's eyes. Slowly she ran her tongue across her lower lip, moistening it. She felt the familiar charge of electricity shoot through her as Montoya returned her gaze, that old familiar sense of power as she realized he had taken the bait and she was in control.

He wanted her. She could see it in his eyes. She could almost smell the lust that poured forth as a light film of sweat broke out on his forehead.

She'd expected no less.

From the corner of her eye, Janie saw Montoya's confident grin. She forced herself to blush and turn away in innocent girlish embarrassment. Then smiling shyly back, she returned her eyes to his.

Janie Brewer had no doubt that Juan Montoya would be hers before the night was over. She only wished it was Rance Pollock who sat watching her with such total infatuation.

LIGHT MOISTURE gathered on the Buick's windshield as Bolan crossed the city limits of Nuevo Laredo. He ignored the wipers. Mixing the drizzle with dust from the Mexican back roads would only decrease visibility further.

Next to him, Buddy Taylor examined the M-16 on his lap. Another in the endless stream of cigarettes hung from his mouth, and occasional raspy coughs were the only sounds he made. Bolan was grateful. It was a pleasant change from the usual blustering that flew from Taylor's lips.

In the rearview mirror, he saw Jackson staring dully at the countryside. The man's bottom lip hung open beneath the erratic mass of hairs over his mouth. Bolan shook his head.

Great guys to go into battle with.

He'd part company with them soon, though, if only temporarily. He neither needed nor wanted the two men with him in Bogotá and would send them back to the States to wait.

The phone call from Janie had altered his plan of attack.

She had established herself quickly in the Colombian capital, and had already gathered bits and pieces of valuable information. She had even learned that a meeting of the cartel's elite was about to take place, and would have the details by the time he arrived.

Bolan watched Taylor hold the stub of a cigarette against the end of the fresh one stuck in his mouth. The Executioner and Grimaldi would take off for Colombia just as soon as the loose ends at the Rodriguez ranch were tied up. The rest of the strike sites in Mexico would have to be put on hold.

There was no point in fishing for scattered minnows when the sharks were gathering.

Bolan was impressed with the speed with which Janie had gained the Colombian general's confidence, and her timely call to the phone booth in the parking garage had proved her dependability. But the warrior saw trouble looming ahead in another form, from an angle he couldn't have anticipated.

Janie was falling for him.

He had suspected it the last few times they'd talked, and the phone call from Bogotá had confirmed his suspicions. The tone of the woman's voice and the almost apologetic way she reported Montoya's pillow talk had erased all doubts from his mind.

Bolan's affection for the likable young woman was platonic. He recognized Janie as the unknowing victim that she was, the end result of a girlish dream of stardom never achieved. She had unwittingly traded the important things in life for the superficial.

Janie had mistaken that affection for another type of love.

There was no easy answer to the situation. His only course was to resolve the matter as quickly and painlessly as possible when he got to Bogotá.

As the rain fell harder and lightning flashed in the distance, the Executioner turned onto a pitted blacktop road. He systematically took mental inventory of his weapons. The Beretta rode snugly under his left arm, its big partner resting in hip leather on the other side. His black combat suit bore extra magazines for the subgun and both pistols. A Gerber Mark II Survival/ Attack blade and a double row of fragmentation grenades hung from the battle harness crisscrossing Bolan's chest.

Insufficient armament wouldn't necessitate a retreat from the ranch. Not this time.

Bolan watched Taylor stub the cigarette butt in the ashtray as the black sky thundered and the rain poured down. He switched the wipers on high as he turned up the dirt drive to the ranch house, hoping the natural camouflage of the rainstorm would help conceal their arrival.

"Fasten your seat belts," Bolan reminded the two men.

Taylor looked up and frowned. "Why?"

The Executioner snapped his own belt into place as he floored the accelerator and sloshed through the muddy approach. "I don't have time for questions, Taylor. Just do what I tell you."

As they neared the house, Bolan cut the wheel hard to the left and cut across the lawn to the rear. They skidded to a halt, mud and grass flying beneath the wheels. The warrior threw the transmission into neutral, gunned the engine twice, then slammed it into Drive.

More mud oozed over the Buick's hood as Bolan stomped on the pedal. The car slid through the rain, smashed through the row of glass doors and burst into the living room. Scraps of glass and aluminum fell over the Executioner's shoulders as he leaped from the vehicle, the Uzi filling his right hand.

A surprised man on the couch fumbled for a pistol that lay on the coffee table. Bolan fired from the hip and a short stutter of 9 mm parabellums punched the man back against the cushions.

Bolan saw Taylor and Jackson exit the Buick. Jackson crouched in combat stance while Taylor rolled behind the solid oak wet bar on the far side of the room.

Two gunners raced headlong through the hall door. Bolan's Uzi cut down the first man in midstride, while Jackson poured a steady stream of .223s into the second.

The Executioner took position near the door, his back against the wall. He raised the Uzi, expecting more resistance from the household guard.

The house was quiet.

Dead quiet.

Noiselessly Bolan pressed along the wall toward the door. He risked a quick glance around the corner, jerking his head back just in time to avoid the shotgun blast that tore the door frame from the wall.

The Executioner dropped to the floor and inched his way back to the opening on elbows and thighs. Then, rising to his knees, he fell forward into the doorway. A second load of buckshot exploded above him where his head had appeared moments before.

Bolan fired as he hit the ground. A long-haired, bearded man dropped the shotgun, rebounded off the wall and fell facedown, pools of blood seeping to both sides of his body.

Footsteps crunched on the broken glass behind Bolan. He twisted around to face two wet and muddy gunners as they sprinted into the house.

The first man's weapon blazed as he crossed the threshold, and Bolan took cover behind the front of the Buick. The gunman fired again and Jackson went down, a .45-caliber slug entering and exiting his right bicep.

The Executioner rose as the gunner sent his third round wildly over the wet bar, shattering the mirror. Tapping the Uzi's trigger, Bolan blew three holes in the guy's face.

The second defender spun back through the demolished doors and dived behind the air-conditioning compressor just outside. Bolan moved back to the wall and cautiously approached. He saw the man's feet protruding from where he crouched behind the thin green metal and heard short, heavy gasps for air above the steady hum of the motor.

Bolan showered the compressor housing with 9 mm projectiles. Gray-edged holes drilled through the green paint, and the motor sputtered to a halt. The heavy breathing changed to one final sigh as the gunman fell from cover.

The warrior retraced his steps to where Jackson lay, stunned. Dropping the Uzi, he ripped the shirt from the merc's chest and mounted a crude field bandage to stop the blood flow.

A gunner in jeans and a white shirt burst through from the hallway as Bolan knotted the bandage. The guy had just enough time to raise his revolver before the Executioner drew the Desert Eagle and sent a .44 round into his throat. The shocked gunman dropped to his knees then fell forward, the white shirt turning crimson.

Bolan shoved the big Magnum back into its holster and dragged Jackson to the back seat of the Buick. He was about to begin a search-and-destroy of the house when he remembered Taylor. The man hadn't fired a shot since barricading himself behind the bar.

Moving cautiously to one end of the bar, Bolan drew the Beretta and held it in a two-handed Weaver's grip as he turned the corner.

The M-16 he'd issued Taylor was aimed at his stomach.

The merc's cold black eyes jumped from the Executioner's to the Beretta before he lowered the weapon, his face growing pale with the effort.

"Sorry," he whispered. "Couldn't be sure it was you." The Executioner nodded. He glanced at the rows of bottles behind the bar.

"You planning on helping out, or would you rather stay here and have a drink of two?"

The loose flesh below Taylor's chin wiggled as his lips curled into a sneer. "Couldn't help it," he said. "Got pinned down. It happens to the best of us, you know."

Bolan nodded again. "And the worst. Stay here and look after Jackson. He's out of sight in the car, but he's had it if they happen to find him."

Taylor hesitated. "Want me to come with you?"

"No, I don't. This job is tough enough without baby-sitting you. Just stay here. And out of my way."

The warrior grabbed the Uzi as he crossed the floor and replaced the clip with a fresh load. His gut-level instinct told him the house was empty—that the gunners inside had all been drawn to the firefight downstairs.

But he had to make sure.

Calmly and methodically he checked each room, probing into closets and any place large enough to conceal a man.

In the master bedroom upstairs, he found a trapdoor that led to the attic. With the Uzi pointed upward, he pulled the cord and unfolded the steps.

Bolan fired a short burst through the opening before climbing up the shaky stairs, and just before his head reached the entrance, he extended the Uzi and fired a 360-degree stream throughout the attic. With the light of a small pen-flash he surveyed the musty room. Nothing.

He returned to the living room, where Taylor still hid behind the bar. "I'm going to check the rest of the grounds," he told the man.

Bolan turned his back to the bar and reached into one of the pockets of his combat suit for another 9 mm load. He'd just ejected the near-empty magazine when he heard the metallic thud of an M-16 bolt snap closed behind him. He was starting to turn, when three armed men appeared in the shattered door frame.

The warrior dived to his left, slamming the clip into the subgun as he fell. He heard the crisp crack of .223s and felt the heat as a 3-round burst missed his ear by scant inches.

From behind.

The Executioner rolled behind the couch. Neither Taylor nor the cartel gunners had a clear shot at him. But depending on the penetration capability of the weapons the Mexicans wielded, the couch could become a death trap.

And the .223 rounds in Taylor's M-16 would burrow through the padded fabric like paper.

Bolan heard more cracks from the M-16, but the couch remained unpunctured. Taylor was evidently preoccupied with the enemy. He had finally been forced into action.

But the warrior knew his brief reprieve would end in seconds. Either Taylor or the Mexicans would emerge victorious, and the winner would turn his attention to the man behind the couch.

Bolan plucked a grenade from his battle harness, pulled the pin and hurled the orb over the back of the couch toward the doorway. He placed a hand over his left ear and covered the right with his shoulder, retaining his grip on the Uzi. Then, hearing the muffled explosion, he sprang from concealment.

Two of the men lay dead in the doorway, their bodies shredded by shrapnel. The third was on his knees, spasming in a pool of blood and vomit, hands clutching what remained of his abdomen. A short volley from the Uzi sent him to join his partners in hell.

A soft moan came from behind the bar. Dropping the near-empty subgun, Bolan drew the Desert Eagle and walked cautiously forward. Taylor writhed painfully on the floor, soaked in the various liquors that had splashed from the exploding bottles overhead. A sharp section of the bar's copper trim protruded from his thigh.

"You son of a bitch," Taylor gritted. "You damn near killed me."

He cursed again as the Executioner wrenched the metal from his leg. Bolan tore strips from a bar towel and tossed them to the merc. "It's not deep," he said. "Tie it off."

"You damn near killed me," Taylor repeated. "And after I saved your life."

"After you what?"

"You'd have been dead meat, Pollock, if I hadn't plugged that guy coming in the door."

Bolan stared down at the man. "I'm going to search the rest of the grounds."

"Just don't forget what I did," Taylor said as Bolan walked away. "But what the hell. We're on the same side, right?"

BOLAN SPRINTED from the house to a nearby storage shed and blew the padlock with a round from the Desert Eagle. Empty. Searches of the other outbuildings flushed no more gunmen. Walking back toward the house, he surveyed the road and prairie. The rain had stopped, leaving the roads semisolid rivers of red mud. He saw no sign of reinforcements over the horizon.

Still, someone would arrive soon—police, army or more cartel gunmen. Maybe all three. He had no time to begin the tedious process of searching for the drug cache.

It didn't matter.

The ranch had been given life by money from the death-inducing substance it now concealed. It could die with it.

Bolan found several five-gallon cans of gasoline in the barn. He opened the horse stalls, scurried the animals through the door then emptied one of the cans throughout the building. Leaving a trail of gas through the door, he struck a match and watched as the structure burst into flame.

The Executioner moved rapidly from building to building, leaving a cleansing flame in his wake. He helped Taylor and Jackson into the back seat of a station wagon before scattering gas from the last two cans throughout the ranch house. He drove the station wagon to safety a hundred yards away and jogged back down the road to the house.

Yanking another grenade from his harness, he pulled the pin and sent the steel destroyer crashing through the glass of a window. A moment later he heard the muffled thunder within, and then the house was consumed.

Bolan kept one eye on Taylor as the wagon slid through the mud to the blacktop. The merc leader lighted a cigarette. The stale smoke and his liquor-soaked clothing made the car smell like the last hour of a New Year's Eve party.

"Not a bad piece of work, if I do say so myself," he observed. "Just don't forget, Pollock—I saved your ass back there." He grinned across the front seat, waiting for Bolan's response.

The Executioner didn't answer. Years of battle had taught him that many things happened in the course of a firefight; things that altered the perceptions of men accustomed to the stress. Even experienced warriors sometimes confused the sequence of events.

But that wasn't the case with Bolan. He knew what had happened at the ranch house. More importantly, he knew in *what order* it had happened.

Buddy Taylor had tripped the bolt of the M-16 before the three gunners appeared at the doorway. Although fired in their direction, his rounds had been meant for the Executioner.

It was Bolan he had tried to kill.

5

The faint glow of the flames grew brighter as Bolan fell through the air. He hit the ground running, pulling the lines to gather the chute even before his forward momentum slowed to a walking pace. In the distance he could hear voices.

The warrior tried to distinguish what was being said as he folded the chute. He'd spotted the camp fire during his HALO descent, but he had limited control over where he landed. The mountain winds of the Eastern Cordillera were ever-changing, and although he had maneuvered the lines with the skill that came from years of practice, he had landed less than two hundred yards from the fire.

The Executioner scraped a shallow hole in the ground for the parachute, covered the material with dirt, then rolled a boulder over the top before slinging his equipment pack and Uzi over his shoulders. During the flight, he'd blackened both his face and hands to blend with the tight-fitting combat suit.

It was unlikely that whoever tended the nearby fire had spotted him or the black chute. If they had, he would have known by now.

But he could afford to take no chances.

Cautiously he climbed over the rocks toward the voices. Unfamiliar words drifted through the trees to the soldier's ear—they weren't Spanish. Certainly not the pure Castilian that the inhabitants of Colombia's major cities prided themselves on speaking. More than likely the people at the fire were members of one of the many Indian tribes that still inhabited the mountains. Guambianos, most likely. He was too far south to encounter the fierce Motilones.

But whatever language it was that Bolan now heard, it carried no tone of urgency or excitement and confirmed his suspicion that his entry into Colombia had gone unobserved.

Bolan moved silently at a forty-five-degree angle to the fire, maneuvering to higher ground to get his bearings. Down the mountain, far to the west, he saw the moonlight reflecting off what had to be the Rio Magdelena.

He peeled back the black canvas watch cover, the luminous hands shining an eerie green in the darkness. If he missed the scheduled meeting with Janie in Bogotá, there would be no way to contact her without casting suspicion her way. She had called Bolan just before he and Grimaldi had taken off, advising that Montoya had insisted that she move into his private quarters with him. Trying to contact her there could be disastrous.

The Executioner knew he had to keep the appointment. He glanced again at his watch. He could make it if he started now, and if he took the most direct route.

But that route lay immediately in front of him, through the camp fire and the unknown people who gathered there.

He had studied a topographic map of the area, and the closest alternate route to this mountain pass lay almost ten miles to the west, through the dense jungle of the valley between the Western and Central Cordillera. It would delay his arrival in Bogotá by several hours.

It was simple, really. He didn't have the time.

Concealed by the shadows, the Executioner moved closer until the silhouettes of several small shacks encircling the fire became visible. Two dozen ragged men, women and children sat cross-legged around the flames.

The warrior had come upon a shantytown. The groups of shacks had become more prevalent over the past few years as the economy of Colombia continued to shift, the drug lords of the cartel gaining even more wealth as the hardworking Colombian peasants grew increasingly more destitute.

Bolan heard laughter and watched as a man with a gray beard passed a clay jug to the woman seated next to him. Above the fire, the frail carcass of a goat rotated slowly on a wooden spit, its body the only thing more emaciated than the children and adults who huddled together.

The Executioner moved back slowly until he reached the small clearing where he'd landed, then climbed up a short ledge to a pass above the camp fire. Dropping to all fours, he inched his way past the poverty-stricken band.

He moved on through the mountains, following the path between a stream and the mountain wall to his right. As he knelt to drink from the stream, he felt a cool chill run up his spine.

The Executioner's battle senses went on alert.

He was being stalked.

Bolan rose and peered through the darkness.

Nothing.

Moving cautiously along the path, his eyes searched the darkness, his ears primed for any foreign sound.

A twig snapped on the ridge overhead.

The warrior drew the silenced Beretta from shoulder leather and backed slowly under an overhang, his eyes probing the ridge.

The night remained silent, then from above came the faint sound of quiet, steady breathing. A shadow fell slowly over the edge of the overhang, forming a distinct shape in the stream in front of the Executioner.

Cougar. Puma. Mountain lion.

Whatever you called it, its jaws could crush a man's skull while it ripped the jugular vein from his throat with its razor claws.

Bolan watched as the big cat lowered its head to peer at him under the ledge. The Executioner moved farther back under the overhang, pressing his back against the cold rock for every inch, every split second he could buy before the inevitable happened.

Suddenly the big cat leaped from the ledge, twisting in midair to face its prey, five feet away. Bolan raised the Beretta. The cougar sprang, the powerful muscles of his hind legs contracting, then jetting him forward with the force of a jackhammer.

Bolan acted from instinct, his trigger finger snapshooting a 3-round burst into the snarling cat's mouth. The silenced 9 mm rounds entered the cougar's soft upper palate, then bored up into the brain as the eight-foot mammoth collapsed at the warrior's feet.

The cougar lay paralyzed, his eyes staring blankly up at the stars overhead. Bolan leaned forward and pressed the muzzle of the Beretta against the animal's head and squeezed the trigger, ending its pain.

He moved from under the overhang and took a last look at the valiant animal he had been forced to kill.

Then the man in black disappeared into the night.

IN DOWNTOWN BOGOTÁ'S Plaza Bolívar, Bolan passed book stands and street vendors hawking leatherware, blankets and *ruanas*—the heavy, square ponchos of the northern region. Though it was Colombia's dry season, cloud formations hovering around the mountain peaks that framed the city meant rain wasn't out of the question.

Rested and alert, Bolan had arrived in time to shower, shave and catch a short nap at the Hotel Regina.

A short walk from the center of town, the Regina afforded ample opportunity for Bolan to scout the streets, acquaint himself with the layout of the city and devise escape routes that he hoped would never be needed.

Old colonial buildings appeared between the steel and glass of modern skyscrapers as the soldier checked out the neighborhood. The temperature had dropped to the mid-fifties, giving Bolan good reason for wearing the thin leather jacket that hid his weapons.

He crossed the street to the statue of Simón Bolívar and took a seat on an empty bench. Four brightly lighted water fountains surrounded the statue, their jetting streams flaunting a vivid spectrum of colors as they arched through the air. The soldier watched nonchalantly as a policeman, stomach bouncing over his black Sam Browne belt, passed in front of the bench. The officer gave him a quick once-over, then disappeared into a pastry shop down the street.

Bolan saw Janie a block away, her fiery red hair blowing down and around her face as she approached the plaza. He had mixed feelings about the encounter about to take place. The Executioner needed to know the time and location of the meeting of high-ranking cartel members in order to cut a deep swath through the hierarchy of the organization, but if his assumption that

Janie was falling in love with him was true, then he'd have no choice but to set the record straight.

Janie had changed. She had learned to respect herself, and Bolan had no desire to do anything that might reverse that transformation. But he couldn't in good conscience lead her on. The last thing on earth he wanted to do was hurt the woman. But so far no one had invented a method of telling someone that their love wasn't reciprocated without shattering their dreams.

Janie looked up as he approached, the smile on her face erasing all hope that he'd been wrong in his perception of her feelings.

"Hello, Rance," she said. Her voice held no trace of the cheap seductress he'd first met in Yuma.

Bolan smiled. "You hungry?"

"Famished," she replied, smiling in turn.

He led her to a street vendor and bought four tamales, handing her two. "Come on," he said. "We'll eat while we walk. That'll attract less attention."

They had started down the street when they heard a scream behind them. Bolan turned in time to see a tall, gangly man in his late teens rip a handbag from the grip of an elderly woman.

The Executioner resisted the impulse to race after the kid. The last thing he needed at this point was the attention of the local police.

But as the thief backhanded his victim to the pavement, Bolan knew he couldn't stand idly by.

The purse snatcher turned from the old woman and sprinted down the sidewalk, directly toward the Executioner.

The overweight cop who'd eyed Bolan earlier exited the pastry shop as the purse snatcher ran past. Dropping the cardboard box he carried, he thrust a whistle into his mouth and gave chase, losing ground with every step.

Bolan waited until the man with the purse was two yards away, then stepped in front of him and lifted a knee.

The thief's momentum carried him forward before he could stop. He let out a high-pitched scream as he impacted on Bolan's knee, then fell to the ground on his side, both hands clasping his groin.

Bolan waited as the fat cop puffed his way to the man on the sidewalk and pulled a set of handcuffs from his belt.

"*¿Norteamericano?*" he asked, looking up quizzically.

Bolan nodded.

"You must—" the cop fumbled for the word "—you must wait." The officer rolled the moaning thief onto his stomach and dropped to both knees in the center of the man's back, eliciting an even sharper scream than Bolan's knee had produced.

A small crowd had gathered, and while the policeman struggled to get the handcuffs on his prisoner, Bolan seized Janie's arm and led her to the corner. Crossing quickly against the light, they cut four blocks over to the corner of Calle Catorce and the busy Avenida Jiminez before flagging down a cab.

"Monserrate," Bolan told the driver as he and Janie slid into the back seat.

They remained silent during the short ride to the summit of the mountain. Bolan tipped the cabbie and he and Janie walked to the train of cable cars. He watched the attendant help Janie on board, then took the seat across from her in the small cabin. The car jerked erratically as the motor kicked into gear, then slowed to a steady swing, adjusting itself to the difference in Bolan's and Janie's weight.

The warrior looked at the young woman seated across from him as they rose into the air. "You've found out where and when?" he asked.

Janie nodded. She opened her purse, withdrew a folded sheet of paper and extended it across the cable car.

Bolan unfolded the paper. Janie had drawn a map of the layout of a small café and lodging area. His eyes fell to the bottom of the page: Casa Tarragona, La Boquilla.

"It's a little country inn a few miles east of Cartagena," Janie said. "Just before you get to La Boquilla."

"Who and when?" Bolan asked.

"Tomorrow. It sounds like they're coming from all over. All the bigwigs from Bogotá, Medellín, Cali." Janie let a short laugh escape her lips. "It seems they're concerned about some Americans who ripped off a plane that had been loaded with cocaine, and some other American who raised hell at the same ranch. Then came back and did it again."

"He's not finished yet."

"Well, you've confused them royally. They can't figure out if you and the Vampire Bats are working together or if they're getting hit by two separate groups at the same time. The Bats, they figure they can handle. It's this tall, dark stranger who has them worried."

"I've been wondering myself whether Taylor and I are really working together," Bolan confided. "I don't trust your friend."

Janie's face colored, and she stared at the floor of the cable car. "He's not my friend. Not anymore.'

Bolan nodded, wishing he'd phrased the statement differently. He refolded the map and dropped it into his jacket pocket. "What time?" he asked.

"What?"

"What time is the meeting tomorrow?"

Janie raised her eyes slightly. "Montoya is leaving at noon for Cartagena. Casa Tarragona is only about fifteen minutes from the airport. I'm going with him."

Bolan frowned. "Any way for you to get out of it? There's bound to be a lot of gunfire."

Janie shook her head. "Not without just coming out and saying no, and that's liable to make him wonder what's going on." She stared at the wall of the cable car, still avoiding Bolan's eyes. "It would be really out of character for the role I've been playing."

Bolan glanced out the window at the red-roofed city of Bogotá and the plains that stretched beyond. The cable car ground to a halt as they reached the top, and he helped Janie out of the vehicle.

They passed the convent and the reconstruction of a Bogotá street of 1887 before finding an empty table at the picnic grounds behind the church.

"There's something else we need to discuss," Bolan said as they sat down. "Janie, I—"

She reached across the table and pressed a finger against his lips. "Let me talk for just a minute. Then we'll see if you still need to say what you were going to. Okay?"

Bolan nodded.

She smiled up at him. "I know you're afraid I've fallen in love with you. I have, I guess. But don't worry, I'm not asking for anything from you. Not even for you to return that love."

"It's not—"

"Shh," Janie whispered. "You promised." She crossed her arms across her chest. "I don't expect you to love me, Rance. It's enough that I can love you. Do you see? It's proved to me that I'm still capable of love, and that's something I was beginning to be afraid I'd lost somewhere down the line. Thanks for treating me so well. It's been a long time since a man looked at me and saw anything I had to offer except the obvious."

Bolan started to speak, then waited.

"Anyway, I don't expect to see you again after today. So it's important to me that you know what I've decided to do." She paused, then continued. "When this is over, I'll go back to the States, of course. I've got a sister in New York City who's offered to let me move in, and I plan to find a university in the area where I can finish my teaching degree."

"No more show business?" Bolan asked.

Janie grinned mischievously. "I don't plan to give up acting—that's why I decided on New York. But I've got to face reality. The fact is that I may never make it. And from now on I want something better to fall back on other than my back."

They rode down the mountain in silence. When they reached the bottom, Bolan said, "Find some way to get out of going tomorrow. There's no point in it. I've got everything I need to know."

Janie shook her head. "It'll look too strange. Don't worry. He won't want me at the meeting, anyway. This is a macho bunch of guys, you know. They'll send us 'girls' off to buy panty hose or something."

Bolan reached in his pocket and pulled out a roll of bills. Peeling several from the top, he pressed them into Janie's hand. "When they do, you take the first flight from Cartagena. The first one to anywhere."

"I will."

The warrior walked her to a row of cabs. He opened the door, then closed it behind her.

Janie smiled up at him through the open window.

"I'm serious," Bolan told her. "You get out of there at the first opportunity. There's no point in taking chances—I don't need you anymore."

Janie's smile faded slightly. "You never did," she said sadly. Then her eyes twinkled with new hope. "But somebody will. Sooner or later. Somebody will need me."

Bolan nodded as he watched the cab round a curve and disappear. Then he glanced at his watch. Time to prepare for battle.

A GENTLE BREEZE rustled the leaves of scattered palm trees as the Executioner made his way over tangled roots in the mangrove swamp. The faint sounds of dancing drifted to his position from the streets of the small fishing village a half mile in the distance.

The warrior peered through the gnarled branches at the country inn that stood in the clearing fifty yards away. Cars had been arriving since dusk, and the cocktail hour would soon be over. Then the meeting of the most powerful drug lords in the Western Hemisphere would commence.

Bolan ran a final check of his equipment. Six fragmentation grenades hung from his battle harness; the .44 Desert Eagle rode leather on his right thigh, a row of magazines for the weapon flanking it front and back on his web belt; the Beretta 93-R silencer-equipped and ready to perform its quiet duties, was sheathed in the shoulder holster under Bolan's left arm. Extra magazines for the Beretta hung from the same rig on the other, balancing out the weight of the heavy automatic.

The backpack held extra reloads for the subgun and various other items that the soldier might or might not need. With the Uzi gripped in both hands, Bolan knelt, then leaned forward onto his stomach and slid on his elbows to the edge of the trees.

He pulled an infrared night vision scope from his pack and began a systematic scan of the grounds, counting fourteen vehicles parked in front of the inn. Six were Rolls-Royces, the rest Cadillacs and Lincolns. One lone army jeep with a .50-caliber machine gun mounted between the seats sat conspicuously among the luxury cars.

A sentry was posted at each end of the four corners of the grounds, two more at the front door and another pair at the inn's back.

The Executioner moved silently through the mangroves to the edge of the swamp farthest from the front door. He watched the sentry light a cigarette and gaze overhead at the stars. Bolan moved slowly, tugging the Beretta from his shoulder rig and setting the safety on semiauto, then sighted down the barrel. A soft tug on the trigger sent both the guard and his Heckler & Koch G-3 tumbling quietly to the ground.

Bolan maneuvered through the trees, circling the house and taking out another of the perimeter guards. He moved on to the edge of the clearing where the third guard paced nervously up and down the narrow drive to the road. The warrior waited until the man's steps brought him within two feet of his position, then sent a hushed 9 mm hollowpoint through the guy's temple.

Bolan doubled back through the trees to where the last guard paced his beat. As though alerted by some sixth sense, the man turned suddenly and squinted into the darkness as he brought a pump action shotgun up to his shoulder.

The Beretta spit two rounds into the man's chest, the sound of their impact on human flesh far louder than the noise-suppressed weapon itself.

Four down. Four to go.

Then the real battle could begin.

Bolan crawled his way out of the clearing to the cover provided by a stilt-mounted gazebo behind the inn. He watched through the night scope as one of the guards on the back porch glanced around nervously, pulled a flask from his back pocket and took a drink. He could see the anticipation on the other guard's face as he waited for his turn.

As the second guard tipped the flask upward, the Executioner sank a round between his eyes, then dropped the guy's partner with a double tap to the throat and chest.

Bolan moved swiftly now, sprinting the short distance that remained between him and the inn. On the back porch he crouched in the shadows, surveying his position to the rear.

No guards were left behind the inn. At least none who were in any shape to sound the alarm.

Bolan stepped over the bodies on the porch and raised his eyes to the window in the back door. Easing the door open as quietly as possible, he slid through the opening and into what appeared to be a storage room. Taking temporary refuge behind a stack of boxes, he took advantage of the moment to load a fresh clip into the 93-R.

From somewhere in the front of the building came the low hum of voices.

Bolan slid noiselessly to one of two doors leading from the room and pressed his ear against its hollow core. He could hear the clinking of dishes being stacked and the splash of what must have been dishwater. The kitchen.

The sound of voices at the second door was markedly louder, and the Executioner dropped to the floor to look into the narrow strip of light that flowed through the crack at the bottom of the door.

At the end of a deserted hall another door was cracked open a few inches. Uzi gripped in his right hand, Bolan opened the door and inched down the hallway. His backpack made a soft swoosh against the rough wood paneling as he crept toward the opening.

Through the door he heard a weathered voice addressing the assembly in Spanish.

"...so the overall damage is minimal," the voice said. "But it must be stopped. What concerns us most is the identity of the man who appears to have been working independently of the group known as the Vampire Bats. They, by the way, are being located and dealt with even as we speak."

Bolan paused to listen. He might as well gather whatever information he could. The members of the cartel wouldn't be able to provide much when he finished here tonight.

He drew the Beretta and held it at his side. The meeting was underway, and there was little chance he'd be discovered in the hall. But if someone did find him, a 9 mm slug would go a long way in silencing the guy.

"As you are aware," the voice continued, "recent internal developments in Panama have caused us concern over Noriega's reliability. He's faced with problems that occupy his time...and concentration, a commodity I'm afraid is in limited supply."

Bolan heard polite laughter ripple through the room.

"He'll fall, one way or another, sooner or later," the voice continued, "and we don't intend to fall with him. Therefore, we can no longer depend on the Panamanians to protect our shipments. I've arranged for other escort...by a gentleman who has proved his reliability over the years and has his own reasons for desiring to see us import cocaine into the United States. It's a name with which you are all familiar." The speaker paused. "Fidel Castro."

There were murmurs, and then a new voice broke in. "General, there's a phone call."

"I left orders that I wasn't to be interrupted," came the angry reply.

"I'm sorry, but it's an emergency."

Whispers came from the dining room as the rest of the cartel honchos awaited Montoya's return. Bolan shifted the Uzi into forward carry position on the sling.

He'd heard enough. As soon as Montoya returned, the Executioner would strike.

He was about to reholster the Beretta when the door to the dining hall swung open and a heavyset man with a light pencil mustache froze in midstride. As a hand moved under his coat, he screamed, "General!"

Bolan fired a 3-round burst into the man's open mouth then shoved him back into the room and out of the way. He jammed the gun into the shoulder rig as he crossed the threshold.

A dozen men sat around an elaborately set table, their eyes wide in shock as the darkly dressed warrior burst into the room. A bald man with a Zapata mustache was in the process of raising a gold-plated goblet, his hand poised halfway between the table and his lips.

The Executioner's first discharge from the Uzi streaked through the goblet and into the man's face and neck. He then turned the subgun on a drug lord in a light cotton suit. As the man shoved back from the table, he caught a long burst of 9 mm fire in the stomach and chest. His legs kicked out reflexively, striking the table and scattering food and dishes throughout the room.

The Executioner sensed the movement behind him more than he heard it. He pivoted smoothly, squeezing the trigger as he turned and coughing a stream of fast-flying rounds into a man who'd approached from the kitchen. The gunner's eyes rolled back in his head as he dropped a sawed-off shotgun and collapsed to his knees before falling forward in death.

As the rest of the men scrambled for cover, Bolan scanned the room for Montoya. The general had disappeared.

Bolan dived to the floor as a tall man with a full beard fired a Browning BDA .380, the 9 mm rounds sailing over his back as he fell. Twisting around as he hit, the Executioner squeezed the Uzi's trigger and ended the assault.

The warrior rolled under the dining table where several of the drug lords had taken refuge. He emptied the remainder of the Uzi's magazine, spraying left to right as the crouched bodies toppled to the floor.

As he ejected the clip, the Executioner saw a hand extend a Taurus .38 under the table and fire blindly. Drawing the Desert Eagle, he fired a .44 Magnum round through the tabletop. The .38 hit the floor a second before a bleeding body.

Peering through the tangled arms and legs beneath the table, Bolan could see the open doorway that led to the front of the inn. A man entered the foyer from a side room visible from the waist down. Then a woman's white, high-heeled shoes and nylon-hosed calves became visible. The man seemed to be dragging her away.

Bolan slid from under the table and started to rise, ducking as a burst of automatic fire tore into the Sheetrock behind him.

He heard the metallic clicks as the gunner ejected his empty magazine and in the short pause between fire, a woman's frightened voice screamed, "Rance!"

Janie Brewer.

Bolan rose from cover and the Desert Eagle jumped twice in his hand, the massive .44 rounds punching the last drug lord against the wall before he slumped lifelessly to the ground.

The Executioner bolted toward the foyer as Montoya raced across the front yard with Janie in tow. He was stopped at the front door by gunfire from the two sentries who were still stationed there. As Bolan dropped to the floor, he saw Montoya grasp a handful of Janie's flaming red hair and throw her into a black Rolls-Royce.

He shoved a fresh magazine up the Uzi's grip and fired at the guards through the closed screen door. The first man went down with blood jetting from his abdomen and thighs. His partner took cover behind a royal palm in the front yard, the MAC-11 machine pistol he held extended around the mammoth trunk.

He yanked a fragmentation grenade from his battle harness, pulled the pin and tossed the explosive through the tattered screen. The grenade hit the ground next to the tree and rolled three feet before exploding, driving shrapnel through the guard's body. Bolan rose and peered through the door in time to see the lights of the Rolls turn onto the highway toward Cartagena.

He hit the floor once more as the first .50-caliber rounds struck the front of the house—the jeep. Montoya's armed escort had stayed behind to eliminate the threat and give his master time to escape.

The Executioner rolled onto his back, the Uzi barrel aiming upward at the overhead lamp in the foyer. A quick round eliminated the light and Bolan's next shot, back into the dining room, canceled the illumination behind him.

Bolan crawled to a nearby window as .50-caliber projectiles continued to cut the air over his head, his hand moving instinctively to another of the grenades that hung from his chest.

No. He'd need the jeep.

And the big machine gun.

Reaching into the backpack, Bolan produced a flare gun and aimed it through the window. An eerie red light illuminated the grounds outside as he sent the flare crashing through the glass and over the machine gunner's head.

The warrior rose to his knees as the man behind the gun stared upward at the flare in surprise.

Seizing the moment, the Executioner fired a burst through the window into the man's head, neck and chest. He then darted across the lawn, pulled the dead man from behind the gun and jumped into the driver's seat.

On the highway, far in the distance, Bolan saw the lights of the Rolls-Royce disappear over a ridge. He twisted the key, cranking the jeep's engine to life, and floored the accelerator.

6

The ice cubes hit the bottom of the plastic tumbler with a dull clink as Buddy Taylor slammed them into four fingers of Rebel Yell bourbon, splashing half the whisky onto his shirt.

The whole mess had turned to shit, Taylor thought, as he sat back down at the white kitchen table. It should have been easy. He didn't know squat about dealing drugs—but he was prepared to learn. And why shouldn't he be? How often did a man have over three hundred kilos of uncut cocaine dropped in his lap? He could have been rich.

He'd been prepared for that, too.

What he hadn't been prepared for was getting his ass shot off... or his throat slit and his tongue pulled out through the hole.

He should have been able to turn the coke and retire to some tropical island where the native broads went around with their tits hanging out all the time. But that wasn't what had happened. Things had changed. As soon as word of his pilot's murder had reached him he'd had to discard all those plans. Taylor's mind returned briefly to that first day at the Rodriguez ranch. Washington. He should have killed the son of a bitch as soon as he went down.

Taylor downed the bourbon and refilled the glass. By the time he'd thought of shooting Washington himself, he'd been too far away to be effective.

And the bastard had talked. The cartel had discovered who he was, who they all were. The name of the game had become survival.

Taylor took another gulp of the bourbon and listened to Jackson snoring loudly in the living room. Drunken sot. Fuck him.

Buddy Taylor had already decided what to do with *him*.

Survival, yeah, he thought. Well, it still should have been easy. Give the damn stuff to Brognola and let the Feds provide him with a new face and life. But no, the goody-two-shoes son of a bitch wanted more. Take a Justice agent and show him the sites.

Shit. There wasn't any sense in that—no money to be made.

Buddy Taylor shook his head. He'd never understand people like Brognola and Pollock. They were on some quest for the Holy Grail—making the world a better place for women and children.

Bullshit. The world was the way it was because people *wanted* it that way. Nothing these clowns in the white hats ever did would change that.

Taylor stood and walked to the window to gaze out over the plains at the southern Arizona desert.

It wasn't much, this ranch, but he liked it, dammit. He'd lived here four years, ever since his first big payoff recovering planes.

Taylor walked out onto the front porch and felt the hot air against his face. He didn't want to leave the ranch. If things went well in the next twenty-four hours, he wouldn't have to.

The merc returned to the kitchen and refilled the tumbler, then took a seat in the living room by the window. He adjusted the air-conditioning unit so the cool air blew directly against his sweaty face, then turned to stare to Jackson.

The younger man lay half on, half off the frayed couch, an empty bottle of tequila snuggled under his folded arms. Taylor shook his head.

Well, things had changed again, and this time it looked like it was for the better. He downed the rest of his bourbon and reflected on the call he'd gotten from Valdez.

Somewhere along the line the Cuban had picked up the fact that Fidel Castro himself would be providing safe passage for the cartel's drug shipments to the States. Castro's minister of defense, Raul Castillo, was staying at the resort right now, finalizing arrangements. Valdez had taken him bone fishing the last two days.

The little greaser was in seventh heaven. He had a plan that he believed would return him to the good graces of Alpha 66 and allow him to play devoted-soldier-to-the-cause again.

Taylor pulled a plug of tobacco from the hip pocket of his khakis and bit off a chunk. He hooked a boot around the brass spittoon at his feet and pulled it between his legs.

Jackson rolled off the couch and hit the floor, his glazed eyes opening momentarily before closing in sleep once more.

Valdez's change in plans had altered his own, Taylor thought. He was sick of this whole business and convinced that if Pollock didn't get him killed somewhere along the line, then Brognola would relent on the Witness Protection thing.

No, he'd been wrong to get into this in the first place. He stood a better chance of surviving on his own.

Taylor looked at his watch. Valdez should have already kidnapped Castillo. It shouldn't be a hard snatch to make. It would consist merely of getting far enough away from land so that gunshots couldn't be heard. Put a few surprise holes in Raul's bodyguards, feed them to the fish and he'd be home free. Then all he had to do was chart a course across the Gulf of California.

Valdez was expecting to meet Taylor and Jackson in Mazatlán with the plane that would transport Raul the rest of the way to Florida—to the glorious reception he was sure awaited when he arrived with his captive.

Taylor spit tobacco juice at the crusty bowl of the spittoon and missed. Valdez had assured him that Alpha 66 would pay handsomely for Raul. He didn't know how much the reward would be, but it would be worth their time and trouble. He and Jackson were welcome to split the money—Valdez would be working not for money but for his homeland.

Shit.

Well, Buddy Taylor didn't know how much money they'd receive, either. But he knew it would be twice as much if he didn't have to split it with Jackson. And he knew that it didn't take three men to fly a bound prisoner to Florida.

Taylor watched the man on the floor from the corner of his eye as tobacco juice dripped from his lips into the spittoon.

He had just two things left to do before he flew off to Mazatlán and then Florida. Returning the cocaine would have to wait until tomorrow when the cartel representatives arrived, but he could get the other task out of the way right now.

Taylor thought of Rance Pollock as he crossed the living room to the bedroom and lifted the .45 from the top of the dresser. The cartel had appreciated the tip. That—and his offer to return the coke—was what would keep him alive.

And Rance Pollock was in for a hell of a surprise when he went after Montoya.

That was another concession. He'd finally seen the last of this lily-white knight.

Returning to the living room, Buddy Taylor stood over Jackson, who had rolled facedown on the hardwood floor. He pressed the .45 against the back of the younger merc's head and without a moment of regret pulled the trigger.

BOLAN HAD DRIVEN four miles down the winding coastal road when he rounded the curve and saw the roadblock. Spanning the highway, nose-to-nose, were two police cars. Parked in the ditch on both sides were two more. Montoya must have radioed ahead.

The Executioner reached back and grabbed the grip of the .50 caliber machine gun, positioning the barrel over the windshield. Pressing down with his index finger in this awkward position, he sent a barrage of half-inch missiles over the heads of the eight Colombian cops who had rallied to the cause.

He smiled grimly as the uniformed officers scampered from the cars to the safety of the ditch.

Bolan had no intentions of harming either Colombian cops or soldiers—they were acting on orders, and for all they knew, protecting their general. Chances were slim that they were involved in any way with the business of the cartel.

The warrior pressed down again on the trigger, sending more rounds flying harmlessly toward the men, then dropped the gun and grasped the wheel with both hands as the jeep smashed into the spot where the bumpers of the police cars touched. The two vehicles spun back and away from the jeep, opening like gates, and the Executioner passed through.

Bolan heard scattered shots behind him as he raced out of there, intent on catching up with Montoya and Janie.

A mile and a half later he slowed at a fork in the road. The left-hand route led south to the village of Sincelejo, according to the sign. The fork to the right continued on past the airport to Cartagena. Bolan twisted the wheel to the right and stomped hard on the accelerator. For a brief moment, far in the distance, he saw the faint glow of taillights before they disappeared.

The warrior sped through the night, his right foot alternating between gas pedal and brake as he navigated the bends in the oceanside road.

He was less than a mile from the airport when he spotted the Rolls-Royce nearing the gate in the airport's perimeter fence. Flooring the gas, his eyes scanned ahead for the resistance he knew he was about to meet.

He wasn't disappointed.

A hail of .223s sailed around the jeep like a swarm of bees as the two gate guards caught sight of him.

Return fire from Bolan's heavy .50-caliber weapon sent them diving for cover, their M-16s falling to the ground.

The Rolls charged through the open gate with Bolan in hot pursuit, his hand steady on the machine gun as two more security men swung the gate closed.

Montoya's car continued onto the runway, and Bolan watched as it turned toward a Boeing 727-100. Even in the distance, the Executioner could hear the roar as the plane's massive engines warmed up.

Across the runway on the far side of the grounds, Bolan could barely make out more uniformed men as they exited a small building carrying submachine guns and assault rifles.

One of the guards was trying to secure a heavy chain around the gate as Bolan neared. The Executioner saw his trembling hands and the strain in his face as he fumbled with the padlock. Pressing down on the machine gun's trigger-button, Bolan sent a steady stream of .50-caliber discouragers a foot to his left. The man dived clear a split second before the jeep rammed the gate, the doors bursting open as the vehicle crossed into the airport grounds.

The collision slowed the jeep. The Executioner downshifted and floored the accelerator to regain speed as he watched Montoya and two other men drag Janie from the Rolls toward the steps of the 727.

Bolan calculated the distance that separated him from Janie and Montoya.

He'd never make it in time.

The hinges of the big machine gun's swivel stand squeaked as Bolan swung the barrel into position once more. He squinted through the darkness at the distant figures, still tiny across the airport grounds.

There was no way; they were too far away. It would be impossible to use the sights on the big gun and steer the jeep at the same time.

He'd gotten by "hip shooting" at the roadblock and gate, but in both those situations there had been a wide margin for error. Precise shot placement hadn't been vital.

If he threw a wild round now, Bolan knew he stood a good chance of sending one of the heavy, half-inch slugs through the body of Janie Brewer.

Bolan raced desperately across the tarmac, hoping to close the gap so a tire shot could be safely attempted. His fist tightened on the gun's grip as he saw Montoya, Janie and the other two men mount the ramp. Janie's dyed hair shone a fiery crimson in the light over the door before she disappeared inside, followed by Montoya. Then his head shot back through the opening, an evil, mocking grin covering his face before he closed the door behind him.

Scattered small-arms fire sailed past the Executioner's head from the oncoming convoy of security men. He swung the big machine gun their way, sending short, choppy bursts to the sides and over their heads.

The vehicles slowed, the men inside evidently not anxious to tackle the big weapon.

Bolan swung the barrel back over the windshield and pressed lightly on the trigger-button, sending a few tentative rounds toward the taxiing plane. His fire fell short.

As the gap continued to close, the Executioner altered his angle of trajectory.

The next burst of automatic fire flew a half-foot high over the Boeing. Turning onto the runway, the plane faced Bolan's oncoming jeep at a forty-five-degree angle and prepared to take off.

Bolan cut the wheel hard left and bore down on the nose of the aircraft, his finger crushing down the trigger-button and sending a steady stream of .50-caliber projectiles across the runway.

For a brief moment, it appeared as if the jeep and airplane would collide on the runway, then the giant Boeing rose over Bolan's head, its heavy vacuum jerking the machine gun from his grip and threatening to pull him up in its wake as he clung to the steering wheel.

The Executioner hit the brake, spinning neatly into a short 180, and Bolan watched the Boeing rise overhead to the east before dipping a wing and heading back toward the airport. In the light of the full moon, he saw a tiny speck descend through the sky as the airplane continued out over the Atlantic.

The object grew larger as it neared the ground, finally allowing Bolan to distinguish the outlines of a body.

As the horrifying reality set in, Bolan heard the scream.

Janie Brewer hit the runway fifty feet in front of the Executioner's jeep.

FELIPE VALDEZ LIFTED the heavy bucket and let the fish, entrails and heads fall over the rail of the Hatteras 48. He watched as the water around the cartel fishing boat turned pink.

Moments later the first dorsal fin appeared on the horizon.

"Señor Castillo?" he heard the fat bodyguard say behind him. Valdez turned in time to see Raul Castillo accept a stainless steel Ruger Mini-14 from the man. "It's only fitting that the first shark is yours," the fat man finished.

Valdez circled the deck of the Hatteras, dumping chum into the water and watching as more dorsal fins appeared in the distance. Excitement gleamed from the eyes of Castillo and the other men as they pulled assault rifles from hard cases and waited as the sharks neared the bait.

The little Cuban descended the steps to the galley and opened the steaming iron pot of paella that the lodge chef had prepared for the trip. When he'd ladled out five dishes of the saffron-seasoned fish and rice, he pulled a small vial from his khaki pants.

"A little extra seasoning, perhaps, Raul?" he said under his breath. "Yes? Good. You'll enjoy it. It's very relaxing. At first."

Valdez poured ground Valium tablets onto each of the five plates and mixed the powder in with the food. The Valium wasn't tasteless, but the saffron would easily mask its bitterness.

Overhead he heard the first shots ring out. Valdez shook his head. It was senseless, a waste. Killing for mere pleasure was foreign to him.

Killing for a purpose—that was another story.

The mass destruction of sharks for sport was a grand example of the way these men had run Cuba since the revolution.

Life, of all types, was cheap.

Valdez placed the metal covers over the plates before carrying them topside. When he reached the deck, he was met by five grinning faces, relaxing and chatting while they reloaded their weapons.

"Martinez!" the fat bodyguard commanded. "More chum."

Valdez lowered his head in subservience. "Pardon, sir," he said. "But the sharks *themselves* are now chum. Others will come to feed off them."

The fat bodyguard's chest puffed out in embarrassment. Valdez laughed to himself. This type of man never minded being wrong—as long as no one noticed.

Valdez spoke quickly to change the subject. "Perhaps you would like to dine now," he said. "The sharks will be here long after we are gone. But the paella will soon be cold."

The fat man's eyes filled with greed as the five men gathered around the deck table, waiting for Castillo to sit.

Valdez set a plate in front of each man and removed the cover before going below to one of the staterooms. He lowered himself on one of the berths and pulled a whetstone from his back pocket. He pulled the long Bowie knife from the sheath on his belt and slid it over the coarse edge.

It should take no longer than a few minutes. Depending on how fast they ate, and each individual's size, the men should soon be sleeping.

The fat one might take longer, Valdez thought. But he'd probably eat more, and faster than the rest, compensating for any advantage his lard might give him.

Valdez felt the nausea rise in his belly as he pictured the scene that was about to unfold. It was terrible beyond belief. Sometimes he was ashamed that such plans even occurred to him.

Then the poetic justice of the thing swept over him, and the little Cuban realized nothing he could do would ever outweigh the crimes these men had committed.

Predators should fall to other predators.

Through the hatch, Valdez heard a body hit the deck. Anxious speech drifted downward to the stateroom and then a weak voice called, "Martinez . . . you . . ."

Valdez closed and locked the door to the stateroom. He moved against the wall behind the bed, the Bowie knife gripped by the blade, ready to be hurled at any of the men who might still be able to enter the room.

No one came.

The little Cuban waited until he was sure the Valium had taken effect before climbing the ladder.

Raul Castillo and the four other Cubans lay unconscious on the deck. The fat bodyguard had gotten his .357 halfway out of the holster. Valdez took the revolver and searched the other men, taking their weapons and tossing them into a pile by the hatch. In the pocket of a guard with a thick, drooping mustache, he found a North American Arms .22 Magnum minirevolver. He stuck it into his waistband.

He went below and opened the refrigerator door, removing a hypodermic needle and several vials of liquid.

The cartel resort's manager had a heart condition, and it had been one of Valdez's duties to make certain that an adequate supply of adrenaline was always on board.

It had been irritating to the little Cuban, just another case of the *peón* serving the *padrón*. But it would come in handy now, and he wouldn't have to wait for the Valium to wear off.

Grabbing a roll of wire, Valdez returned to the deck and bound each man's wrists and ankles. Tiny trickles of blood seeped from the spots where the thin wire sliced into their flesh. He dragged each sleeping body to the rail before injecting the men with adrenaline. Valdez moved to one of the benches on the foredeck and waited as, one by one, the men opened their eyes.

"Martinez?" the fat man said. "What's happening?"

Valdez stood and walked to the man. Then, with surprising strength, the little Cuban grasped the fat man's belt and lifted him over the rail.

He dumped the bloody contents of another chum bucket after the man. Seconds later, the blue water turned crimson as two sharks fought over the screaming Cuban bodyguard.

Then the screams ended.

Valdez stared into the horrified eyes of the next man at the rail. "For crimes against the people of Cuba," he said, "I sentence you to death." He lifted the second man, screaming and kicking, and cast him into the water.

The sharks left what remained of the fat bodyguard, sinking their three-inch teeth into the fresh meat.

Valdez turned to Castillo, who sat bound at the end of the line. "I want you to see it all," he sneered at the man. "Watch carefully. Each one is different, and who knows? Perhaps the stomachs of our finned friends will be full when your turn comes."

The minister of defense's face had turned a pale gray. "You're not Mexican," he whispered.

"No."

"Cuban?"

Valdez didn't bother to answer. He lifted another bucket of blood and fish over the rail and smiled when a dozen more fins approached the boat. "They are hungry, no? Like the people of Cuba."

Tears and mucus had dripped from the nostrils of the mustachioed man, and for a brief moment, Valdez pitied him. Then he pushed such thoughts from his mind.

He glanced at the waters below the boat. They had calmed once more as the sharks finished off whatever flesh was left.

Valdez hurled the man with the mustache after his partners, and suddenly the sea was alive again in a flurry of water and blood.

The last bodyguard screamed, and tried to kick at Valdez with his bound ankles.

The little Cuban stepped back and laughed. "Why not? Why not try? What can I do? Throw you to the sharks?"

"Have mercy!" the kicking man begged, his eyes closed tightly against the future.

Valdez grinned. "Mercy?" he said. "No, friend. Did Raul Castillo have mercy on my father? My sister?" He grasped the legs of the final bodyguard and flipped him over the rail to the flashing teeth below.

The little Cuban turned to the minister, who was whimpering at the boat's bow. He made a futile attempt to cross himself with his wire-bound hands.

"Ah, do you believe that God will save you now?" Valdez taunted. "Is God a member of the Party?" He grabbed Castillo under the armpits and hauled him to his feet, forcing his head over the rail. The sharks had finished devouring the bodyguards and were turning on one another as new dorsal fins continued to appear on every side of the Hatteras.

A high-pitched squeal erupted from the minister's lips.

Laughing, the little Cuban shoved him to the deck on his back. "I have other plans for you," he spit. He watched as his victim's chest heaved in fear.

Raul Castillo looked up into Valdez's eyes, his face a mask of terror. He took another deep breath, then said,

"Nothing will come of this. Nothing except your death, Martinez."

Valdez snorted. He removed his sweat-soaked bandanna and wrung it out over the rail before replacing the damp band on his forehead. He listened to the fishing boat's big engine, the steady rumble calming him as it guided them across the Gulf of California toward Mazatlán.

The little Cuban gathered the bodyguard's weapons into his arms. "My name isn't Martinez," he said.

The CIA faction that advised and aided Alpha 66 was good. The documents they had provided three years ago had stood the inspection of the cartel.

But while the CIA was good, it wasn't perfect. The Mexican passport and other papers hadn't been recalled when he was banished from Alpha 66, and along with his obvious knowledge of fishing and boats, had secured him the trusted position of captain on the cartel lodge's fishing boat.

"Jorge Martinez" had even been trusted with Fidel Castro's right-hand man.

Valdez went below and dropped the guns on the galley table. One of the men had carried a Heckler & Koch 9 mm "squeeze cocker," and Valdez felt the comforting weight as he slid the pancake holster onto his belt.

The little Cuban pulled the .22 minirevolver from his pocket, thumbed the hammer to half cock and removed the cylinder. The weapon held five rimfire Magnums. Valdez reassembled the tiny pistol and stuck it back into his waistband. It would be easier to conceal than a larger gun once they arrived at Mazatlán, and who knew when it might come in handy?

Castillo had regained some of his composure by the time Valdez returned to deck. "So, if your name isn't Martinez," he said, "what is it?"

Valdez stared into the other man's eyes. "You'll find out soon enough."

"There's a saying amongst your American friends," the minister said. "Let's cut through the bullshit. My premier will reward you handsomely for my return."

The little Cuban snorted. "Yes, perhaps I should change course immediately for Cuba. I would receive a warm welcome, no doubt. Perhaps I could be honored as a hero of the revolution?" His light tone changed suddenly to a snarl. "Now, keep quiet unless you are spoken to. It is *I* who am dictator on this boat."

Valdez took a seat on the foredeck and pulled the whetstone from his back pocket. He stroked the Bowie knife along the top. The blade already carried a razor's edge, but the movement relaxed him. He had a great deal yet to do, and he knew he would have to stay calm, would have to keep occupied, to keep from letting his emotions take over. He would have to work at relaxing.

The little Cuban's mind drifted briefly to the only era in his life when he hadn't had to work at relaxing—his childhood in Havana.

He'd practically grown up on his father's fishing boat. Carlos Valdez had been both father and mother to him and his sister. Then the change had come, change in the form of this man's boss, Fidel; change in the form of communism.

As he ran the blade back and forth across the stone, Valdez watched Castillo squinting painfully against the hot sun.

On Valdez's twelfth birthday, he'd arrived at the docks to find his father's boat in the hands of the revolutionaries. He'd never forget the men in green fatigues dragging Carlos Valdez to the jeep and driving away.

He never saw his father again.

The merc wiped the grit from the Bowie blade onto his pants leg. He and his fifteen-year-old sister had joined the ranks of the other war orphans who roamed the streets of Havana, surviving as best they could in the chaos that followed.

Then his sister had found another way to survive.

The hatred and anger he'd carried for more than twenty years filled the little Cuban's heart. He stared at the exposed throat of the man on the deck.

No, not yet. There was more at stake than his own pride, more to be gained than the simple revenge he was owed by this man.

Valdez walked back to the rail and gazed out across the open water. Delivering the chief henchman of the Western Hemisphere's most hated dictator would mean his return to Alpha 66 and the cause that had become his sole reason for living. His past sins would be forgiven.

This devil would be his savior.

Behind him, Valdez heard the minister shift positions, then grunt.

Good. That was what pigs did. Grunt.

"My circulation has stopped," Castillo called.

"Good."

"But the wires are cutting my wrists. Will you loosen them?"

"No." Valdez continued to stare at the ocean.

"Tell me," the voice continued. "How did you leave Cuba? Were you among the criminals and mental patients my premier gave the United States a few years ago?"

Valdez looked back over his shoulder and smiled. "No. When I was seventeen I stole a fishing boat. Your harbor police and shore patrol aren't as clever as you would like to believe."

The merc turned to face his captive. "Do you remember a housekeeper you once had?" he asked.

The man on the deck snorted. "I have had many housekeepers over the years."

"Yes, I'm aware of that. It was quite a joke on the streets of Havana. 'The premier's best friend has another new housekeeper. Or secretary. Or cook.' Always said with a smile. Usually followed by 'And she is even younger than the last.' Or if a family member was present, some attempt at consolation. Such as how much better it was than resorting to the common prostitution many young girls were forced into in those days." Valdez paused, then said quietly, "Her name was Evangelina. She was one of your many housekeepers who also served as your whore."

A leer crossed the captor's face. "As I said, there have been many."

"There will be no more."

"We will see."

Slowly Valdez crossed the deck and slid into the seat above where Castillo lay. He grasped the man by the hair and pulled the face up to his. Methodically Valdez backhanded the man until a thin trickle of blood ran from the corner of the minister's mouth. "My name is Felipe Valdez," he gritted. "Evangelina Valdez was my sister."

A new concern came into the captive's eyes. "Yes," he said. "I remember her, now." He paused, frowning and squinting, and Valdez could see he was considering his next words carefully. "I...loved her very much," he finally said. He watched Valdez anxiously.

The little Cuban felt the hatred and frustration of twenty years suddenly centralize in his chest. He backhanded his captive again, the force of the blow knocking the man from his grasp and back to the deck. Hand trembling, the little Cuban drew the Bowie knife and knelt astride the man's chest. He brought the point of the blade to the minister's throat.

"Don't insult my intelligence," he growled, tears forming in his eyes.

"No," Castillo whimpered. "You must believe me... she escaped."

Valdez grasped the crotch of the minister of defense's baggy fishing pants. Slowly he sliced open the light cotton material. He did the same with the underwear he found below.

With the Bowie's false edge, the little Cuban gently hefted a testicle. He heard Castillo suck in a lungful of air. "Was she good, my sister?" he asked softly. "Did you enjoy her?

"Tell me, what will it be like when you return to Cuba as a eunuch?" Valdez threw back his head, laughing as the wind hit him in the face.

He lifted the other testicle with the knife and leaned forward, staring down at his horrified captive. Castillo's heavy breathing sent the rich odor of a recently smoked Havana cigar to his nostrils and with it the reminder of all this man and his premier had stolen, not just from him, but from all the people of Cuba. Valdez shook his head.

"No!" Castillo screamed. "Your sister is free...she escaped!"

Valdez leaned slightly into the blade and saw a few drops of blood shine in the sunlight on the stainless steel of the Bowie knife. "She did *not* escape," he whispered.

"Yes!" the minister pleaded. "We received intelligence reports later. She was smuggled on board a French freighter...she's free."

Valdez gazed into the terrified eyes below him. They seemed to be somewhere far away, at the end of a long tunnel. The little Cuban felt as if some outside force were guiding his arm as he shifted the Bowie to an ice pick grip and raised it slowly over his head. "There was a hurricane. The ship was lost," he heard himself say.

Like their father before her, his sister had simply vanished.

"No!" the man screamed as the knife descended.

It passed a centimeter from his left ear and wedged in the deck of the Hatteras.

Raul Castillo's eyes were still closed when Valdez wrenched the Bowie from the deck and stood. He took a step away from the cringing man then sent a vicious kick into his exposed groin. The minister screamed again and opened his eyes.

"You will die, you son of a bitch," Valdez promised. "But not yet. You are about to meet some friends of mine. Perhaps you have heard of them. They call themselves Alpha 66."

A new panic covered the face of the man on the deck. He shook his head violently. "Kill me now," he begged.

Valdez chuckled. "It's difficult not to honor your request." He replaced the Bowie in the sheath. "But you will serve certain purposes before you die."

He looked down at the broken man now huddled in a fetal position as he attempted to protect his genitals. He stepped forward and brought his right foot back to kick again, then stopped.

Felipe Valdez walked to the rail and stared vacantly past the bow at the endless miles of water in front of him.

Ahead lay Mazatlán. Then they would fly over the Mexican mainland, before reaching another gulf with waves that rolled very much like the ones he saw before him now.

And somewhere beneath those rolling waves of the Gulf of Mexico, his sister, Evangelina, was finally at peace.

7

The Executioner had no time to linger over the broken body on the runway. Automatic gunfire rang out from both sides of the jeep. Bolan felt the compressed energy as bullets blew past his face. He floored the accelerator and cut the jeep's steering wheel hard to the left.

As he neared the airport's main gate, four regular army vehicles and a dozen Colombian police cars sped up the road to block him off. Bolan hit the brake and skidded the jeep at a forty-five-degree angle. He turned toward the next gate, away from the oncoming militia.

Several more police cars barred his exit.

He cut the wheel again as the closest policemen opened fire. One round struck the steering wheel, shattering the hard plastic. The right half of the wheel crumbled beneath his hand.

He gripped down hard on what was left of the guiding device, forcing the jeep into a sliding U-turn. Stomping hard on the pedal again, the Executioner raced back across the runway toward the opposite side of the field.

His battle senses kicked into high gear as he neared the hangars on the other side of the runway. The warrior couldn't bring himself to kill the Colombian cops and soldiers. For all they knew, Montoya was the honest, progressive chief of the armed forces he portrayed to the media. He didn't publicize the fact that he was also the head of the most notorious drug distribution network in the world.

And the Executioner's trick of firing over his pursuers' heads was wearing thin. It had worked well enough at first, putting a damper on the hue and cry during his initial strike. But the guards had either noticed that no one actually fell under his onslaught, or the arrival of reinforcements had bolstered their courage.

Bolan had to find a different approach, had to devise a way out of the Cartagena airport, through the steadily growing number of soldiers and police that were quickly surrounding him.

And he had to do it fast.

As he crossed the edge of the runway to the grass of the field, the warrior spotted a lone gate at the far corner of the airport. A shadowy row of open-sided hangars led to within thirty yards of the chain-link fence.

From the corner of his eye, he spotted three of the newly arrived Cartagena police cars racing to seal it off.

The Executioner leaned on the gas and turned toward the exit.

The three cars were too far ahead and would reach the gate before him. But it would be a difference of only seconds, and the cars' occupants wouldn't have sufficient time to set up. It would be a moment of tense confusion and fear as they leaped from their vehicles to fire into the oncoming jeep.

Reaching behind, Bolan caught the hot barrel of the .50-caliber machine gun in the crook of his arm and bent it forward. Aiming two feet over the roof line of the cars, he found the trigger with his right hand while his left struggled to control the shattered steering wheel.

He was less than a hundred yards away when the cars screeched to a halt in front of the gate. Gripping the trigger-button, he sent a long volley over the vehicles as the men inside exited and dived for cover.

Bolan squeezed the trigger once more, then leaped from the speeding jeep as he passed the last hangar. The vehicle raced on, hitting two of the hurriedly parked police cars and continued into the fence, stalling to a halt as the Executioner rolled to concealment in the shadows against the building.

Bolan watched as three uniformed men rose from cover and rushed to the fence, M-16s trained on the empty jeep. Their heads swiveled as one when they noticed that the jeep was empty. He heard the excitement in their voices as they turned from the jeep toward the long row of buildings.

But by then the Executioner was inside the open hangar.

The warrior saw a long row of small aircraft and crept behind a 1947 Funk in one of the stalls. He watched as the men walked slowly toward the hangar, weapons at the ready. As they neared, one gunner broke off and circled the building. The other two stopped outside. A muted voice barked orders, and the second man lifted a radio to his lips and whispered into it.

He'd been lucky so far. The three cars racing to secure the gate had contained only the drivers, so he faced only three men. But it would only take minutes for that to change. The radio message would bring dozens more swarming to the hangar.

Bolan inched open the door of the plane and swung up and into the Funk's cockpit. He lowered himself below window level and waited.

Two of the men passed the window, whispering nervously in the darkness.

"He's here, somewhere, Captain," Bolan heard the soft voice say in Spanish. "He can't vanish like a ghost."

"I'm not so sure," a second voice answered.

"Should we check inside the planes?" the first voice asked reluctantly.

"Not yet. We'll wait for the others. Go and check on Domingo."

Bolan heard feet shuffle slowly away and raised his eyes over the edge of of the window. The man who had given the orders stood just outside the Funk, his back to the window.

Careless, Bolan thought. And that would cost him.

The warrior scanned the hangar through the semi-darkness. The two other men were at the opposite end of the long port.

The Executioner reached through the window and encircled the policeman's neck with his arm, his hand covering the mouth. He jerked the man backward against the door of the plane and pressed the silencer of the Beretta against his temple.

The surprised man tried to turn and Bolan shoved the Beretta harder into his skull. "Quiet, now," he said in Spanish.

The Executioner slid from the cockpit, still holding the man through the open door. "I'm going to let you go. Don't make a sound. You do and you're dead. Understand?"

The man nodded.

"Do exactly what I tell you and you'll live," Bolan said, and slid his arm back through the opening. He unslung the M-16 from the officer's shoulder and set it on the seat of the plane. Pulling a Taurus 9 mm auto rifle from the flap holster on the man's hip, he tossed it after the rifle.

Bolan pulled the officer out of sight behind the Funk as a dozen siren-screaming vehicles approached, red lights flashing across the runway. "Order your men out to meet them," he whispered.

"Luis! Domingo! Go and show the others where we are."

Bolan waited until the men had obeyed, then dragged his captive toward the gate behind the hangar. "When we get to your car, I'm going to get on the floor in the back seat. You're going to drive us out of here through the main gate. Slowly. Just like you're going home. Do what I say. I don't want to have to kill you." He paused to let it sink in. "Understand?"

"Perfectly," the officer replied.

Bolan pushed him behind the wheel and slid in the back. He tapped the suppressed Beretta gently on the back of the man's neck as he started the engine. "Remember."

The warrior pressed himself down against the floorboards as the driver passed the oncoming vehicles. They drove, unnoticed in the excitement, back across the airport.

But the Executioner knew that getting through the gate would be another matter. All exits would still be sealed and all vehicles, regardless of markings, would get at least a rudimentary check.

The other officer in the hangar had called the man "Captain," and Bolan had seen the bars on his shoulders as they entered the car. That would help. Some.

But it wouldn't make much difference if the guards at the gate approached the car and saw the Executioner crouching in the back seat.

They left the tarmac and passed several small outbuildings as they neared the gate.

"Pull over," Bolan ordered.

The driver stopped the vehicle next to a storage shed.

"Get out and go to the trunk. Get me a blanket and some other equipment of some kind to cover up with." He glanced quickly down at the black combat suit and assault harness. "And a jacket of some type."

"I'm sorry," the captain said. "I have no blanket."

Bolan cocked the Beretta and pressed it into the man's nape. "You must have forgotten," he said. "There's a blanket back there to cover accident victims when they go into shock."

"Ah, yes," the captain said.

"There's also a shotgun," Bolan added. "Touch that, and I'll put one between your eyes."

The captain got out and opened the trunk. He removed the blanket, a wrinkled raincoat and a ballistic nylon vest as Bolan pressed his forehead against the rear windshield and watched through the crack between the car and trunk lid.

The captain returned to the driver's side and handed the equipment over the seat.

"I'll be defenseless as we go through the gate," Bolan told the man. "I'll be able to hear but not see. You can signal somehow, if you want to. But remember, this gun will be two inches from your heart, behind the seat. I'll pull the trigger with my dying breath, if I have to."

The captain's voice squeaked slightly as he said, "You won't have to."

Bolan slid into the raincoat, covering his weapons. He pulled the blanket over his head and reached from under it, pulling the vest on top to disguise his outline. With any luck, it would look as if the captain had hurriedly loaded his equipment during the excitement.

But luck wasn't always an ally, Bolan reminded himself.

He hadn't been lying when he told the driver he'd be defenseless. It was the weak link in the chain, the calculated risk that always appeared and had to be taken sometime during every mission. The Executioner would be relying on his instinct that the captain believed he would shoot through the thin seat if necessary.

But it was a step he wasn't prepared to take. If the men at the gate checked the vehicle closely, the Executioner would soon be in the hands of the police.

"What should I say?" the captain asked.

"Up to you," Bolan replied. "But you'd better hope it gets us through." He pushed the Beretta forward slightly, shaking the seat as a reminder.

The warrior felt the vehicle slow as they approached the gate.

The moment of truth had arrived.

"Ah, Captain Garza," a voice from outside the car said. "Have they captured the assassin already?"

"Not yet," the man in the front seat said. "But it's only a matter of time. He's in one of the hangars at the far corner of the field."

Bolan heard the first voice again, closer this time. The gate guard had to be leaning on the vehicle now, speaking through the open window. "You have been in a hurry, Captain. You have loaded your equipment as sloppily as I do."

Garza laughed. "Yes, Corporal. It was a fast trip from Cartagena. Perhaps I should put myself on report."

The other man laughed back. "Shall we go ahead and dismantle the blocks at the gates?"

"No, Corporal. Who knows what tricks this madman still has up his sleeve? Wait until he has been secured. Now, let me pass."

Bolan waited until they had driven away before throwing the blanket off. Without speaking, he crawled over the seat next to Garza.

"Where are we going?" the man asked.

"Cartagena," Bolan answered.

They rode in silence until the lights of the coastal town appeared in the distance. Bolan ordered Garza to pull off the road again and saw the fear creep into the captain's eyes.

"Give me your handcuffs," the warrior demanded.

Garza pulled the handcuffs from his belt pouch and handed them across the seat. Bolan slipped them over the man's shaking wrists and pocketed the key.

"Now get out and walk around to the passenger side."

Bolan slid across the seat behind the wheel as Garza took his place. He drove the rest of the way to town and pulled into the deserted parking lot of a supermarket, parking next to a pay phone.

The warrior reached the operator and placed the call to Montoya's estate in Bogotá. He handed the receiver to Garza. "Find out where he is."

"But—"

"Do it." He struck the Beretta in Garza's ribs and pressed his ear against the phone next to the captain's.

"This is Captain of Police Lorenzo Garza, Cartagena," the man said in Spanish. "I must speak to General Montoya immediately."

A female voice answered over the crackling line. "The general is unavailable," she said. "He'll be out of the country for several days. I can let you speak to one of his staff."

Bolan nudged Garza with the Beretta.

"Where has he gone, may I ask?" Garza said.

"I'm sorry. That's classified. There was an attempt on his life this evening."

Garza raised his voice slightly. "Yes, that's what I'm calling about. It's imperative that I speak—"

"I'm sorry—"

Bolan took the phone from Garza and hung up.

He had dropped a coin in the slot when he saw another police car pass. The brake lights flashed as the driver saw the car at the phone booth.

Bolan fished the key from his pocket and pulled the cuffs from Garza's wrists. "I'll be sitting in the back of the car, wearing these." He paused, bringing the Beretta up and under Garza's nose. "And holding this."

Garza nodded silently.

Bolan glanced quickly across the parking lot to where the other police car was crossing to meet them. "Make a phone call," he said.

The Executioner hurried to the back seat while Garza punched numbers into the instrument. Bolan slipped the open cuffs over his wrists and dangled the Beretta between his knees, out of sight.

The other car parked next to them and a bareheaded young officer got out. He stopped halfway to the phone booth and returned for his hat, giving Bolan a surly glance as he walked by.

Bolan half closed his eyes and let his chin fall to his chest.

"Any problem, Captain Garza?" the young cop asked as he neared the booth.

Garza held the receiver to his ear with one hand and waved him away with the other. "Only a troublesome drunk."

The young cop hoisted the Sam Browne belt around his waist. "I'll deliver him for you." He turned toward Bolan.

Bolan saw Garza glance up quickly, then say, "No. I'm on my way to the station now." He hung up the phone and returned to the vehicle.

The young cop shined his flashlight through the window to Bolan's face, then dropped it to the handcuffs between his knees.

The warrior squeezed his calves tighter around the Beretta.

The man with the flashlight nodded and returned to his vehicle.

When he was out of sight, Bolan walked Garza back to the booth.

GRIMALDI WAS WAITING a little over two hundred miles away, across the Venezuelan border in Maracaibo. The Stony Man pilot answered the phone on the second ring.

"I'm in Cartagena," Bolan told him. "There's a little place about fifteen miles east of here. Turbaco. Just south of the mud volcanoes is a flat stretch where you can land. I'll be there in an hour."

"You work fast, Striker," Grimaldi said. "You already finished?"

Janie Brewer's torn and mangled body flashed through the Executioner's mind. He saw Montoya, laughing and taunting as he closed the door of the plane. "I haven't even started yet," he replied and hung up the phone.

Bolan stopped the car halfway between Cartagena and Turbaco. "Here's where you get off," he told Garza.

"You will kill me now, no?" the captain asked. He appeared to have resolved himself to his fate.

"No," Bolan said and watched the relief etch itself into the man's face.

Garza smiled uneasily. "You killed no one at the airport," he said. "Yet, somehow, I cannot believe it was poor aim."

"It was *good* aim."

"Yes. But you would have killed General Montoya had you caught him?"

"Yes. And I will."

Garza frowned. "But...why?" He got out of the car and leaned through the window.

Bolan handed him the handcuff key and shook his head.

Garza nodded. Then the smile vanished and he dropped his eyes to the ground. "I have lost face," he said. "I will return in shame."

"It's better than being dead," Bolan said.

Captain Garza stared the Executioner in the eye. "Somehow, I cannot believe that."

Bolan threw the car in gear and headed toward Turbaco.

He'd never believed it either.

A DUST DEVIL WHIRLED its way across the dry Arizona desert below the ridge where the Executioner lay hidden. He adjusted the center focus on the binoculars and pressed them against his eyebrows. Far across the canyon, he saw two pickup trucks, a car and a Jeep, next to a one-story adobe ranch house.

A hundred feet to the left of the house, Buddy Taylor scooped the last spade of dirt into the hole. The sweating merc had been busy shoveling since Bolan had arrived that morning to set up surveillance.

The Executioner wondered again what Taylor was trying to hide.

The cocaine? It didn't seem likely. The devious mercenary would have stashed it somewhere immediately upon his first return from the Rodriguez ranch. No, this had to be something else. Taylor had been up to something since Bolan had sent him and Jackson back to the U.S. to wait—something *besides* tipping the cartel to the fact that the Executioner was in Colombia, something in addition to the phone call that had allowed Montoya to escape.

Bolan watched as Buddy Taylor leaned the shovel against the house and took a seat in the porch swing beside a stack of firewood.

The Executioner had had plenty of time to think it over. His mind had begun work on the puzzle even as he fought his way from the airport.

It had been obvious that Montoya's emergency phone call had been a tip-off from someone, and the call had given the cartel leader the split second head start he needed to escape.

As he'd flown back to North America with Grimaldi, Bolan had realized that only one man had had both motive and opportunity to make that call.

Taylor had obviously decided to try what Hal Brognola had feared since the beginning. He was now "in bed'' with the cartel. The exchange of the cocaine for his life had been their wedding gifts to each other.

And Janie Brewer had been his dowry.

Bolan continued to watch as Buddy Taylor flipped the pop top off a Budweiser can. Through the powerful 15x60 lenses, he saw a foamy trail run down the stubble on the man's chin and onto his grimy T-shirt.

Bolan fought the urge to reach for the Weatherby Mark V that lay on the rock by his side.

No, he would wait. He needed to ascertain Montoya's whereabouts, and Taylor just might have that information. The two men were equally guilty for Janie's death, and the Executioner was determined they both would pay.

He also needed to determine the location of the hidden cocaine.

There were two reasons the Executioner had set up on the ridge rather than go directly to the house and confront the slovenly merc. First, his initial recon from the ridge had noted the .45 Taylor wore on his hip as he shoveled.

Taylor expected Bolan to be dead. If the Executioner suddenly appeared, the cowardly soldier of fortune was likely to panic and go for the gun, meaning Bolan would be forced to kill him before learning the whereabouts of his stash.

Secondly, if Bolan's gut-level instinct about Taylor cutting a side deal with the cartel was true, then Colombians were bound to arrive soon to reclaim their deadly white powder.

If they didn't come to the ranch itself, then the Executioner would follow Taylor to them. Taylor might know where Montoya was hiding. Then again, he might not. But there was a good chance the cartel men would know where to find their boss.

Far in the distance, Bolan heard grinding gears straining against the bumpy trails. A few minutes later a battered Winnebago pulled into the clearing. The cartel henchmen had known it would take a large vehicle to transport that amount of cocaine. But they hadn't counted on the rough terrain.

Buddy Taylor took several steps off the porch and waited, his hand resting on the grip of the holstered .45.

Two men exited the vehicle, and in the stillness of the canyon, Bolan could make out the faint sound of angry voices. The Winnebago's tall driver gestured dramatically at the dent in the right front bumper.

Taylor shrugged.

More unintelligible words filtered across the canyon as the driver calmed down. Bolan watched as Taylor walked to a jeep, opened the door and motioned for the men to follow. The tall man shook his head as he and his partner returned to their vehicle. Through the binoculars, Bolan saw Taylor frown.

They were obviously on their way to get the cocaine from wherever the merc had hidden it. Why didn't the two gunners want to ride with Taylor and spare their own vehicle further abuse over the rugged southern Arizona wasteland?

The Executioner knew the answer.

He wondered if Taylor did.

The Colombians didn't intend to drive Taylor's jeep back to pick up their vehicle after they got the cocaine. And as soon as they learned the location of the stash, Buddy Taylor would be in no condition to drive it himself.

Or to do anything else.

Bolan grabbed the Weatherby and sprinted to the Land Rover on the trail behind the ridge. He threw off the emergency brake, pushed the stick into neutral and let the vehicle coast silently down the mountain.

An eighth of a mile from the lone road that led to the house, the warrior pulled behind a clump of sagebrush and waited. A few seconds later, Taylor's jeep passed, followed closely by the Winnebago.

Bolan gave them a two-minute head start before he cranked the key in his vehicle's ignition. It would be slow going over these winding trails, and the Executioner had no intention of rounding a curve to find himself bumper-to-bumper with the large recreational vehicle.

As he topped a hill, Bolan spotted the other two vehicles on high ground ahead. Hitting the brake, he waited until they disappeared on the other side.

He crested the next hill and came to a fork in the road. There was no sign of either the jeep or Winnebago.

Bolan parked the Land Rover and jogged back to the top of the hill. Pressing the binoculars to his eyes, he scanned the peaks and gulches in front of him. Just off the left fork, a mile ahead, he saw the dust of the two vehicles as they pulled from the road into a small ravine. A half mile to the right was a tall rise overlooking the area.

There was little chance that they'd see or hear him now, and Bolan's tires spun as he left the road and took off across open country toward the slope.

Circling out of sight behind the hill, he was forced to slow as the grade steepened. Halfway up, he grabbed the Weatherby and abandoned the Land Rover, making his way over rocks and bristly shrubs to the top.

The Executioner squeezed between two jagged boulders on the edge of the ridge. Far below he could see tiny figures. He uncapped the Bausch & Lomb 6x24 target scope atop the Weatherby and pressed the side of the rifle stock against his cheek.

Beyond the cross hairs, he saw Taylor and the two Colombians standing at the mouth of a cave.

The warrior bracketed the taller Colombian between the horizontal lines of the Prismatic Rangefinder and the yardage appeared on the screen: 521. He dialed the bullet-drop knob accordingly as the three men disappeared into the cave. Thirty seconds later they came out, arms loaded with brown packages.

Bolan waited while they made several more trips in and out of the cave before the Colombian driver closed the door and turned to Taylor.

The red-faced mercenary was leaning against his Jeep lighting a cigarette when the short Colombian swung a sling-mounted Ingram MAC-10 from under his jacket. The taller Colombian had circled around the vehicle and now stood behind Taylor, his own gun drawn, ready to take the man in a cross fire.

The merc's mouth dropped open, the cigarette falling to the ground.

Bolan held the cross hair dead on the gunner with the machine pistol and squeezed the rifle's trigger. The heavy Weatherby Magnum echoed throughout the ravine, the recoil pushing the Executioner's shoulder slightly back as he watched through the scope.

The short man's face exploded.

With practiced hands, Bolan worked the bolt, chambering another of the giant rounds.

He swung the cross hairs onto the second gunner, who had turned in the direction of the explosion. The man held his weapon in both hands, jerking first one way and then another as he searched frantically for the sniper.

The Executioner squeezed the trigger once more and another 500-grain projectile left the barrel and found its mark, entering the chest of the Colombian and throwing him backward onto the ground.

Bolan sighted through the scope at Buddy Taylor.

The petrified merc stared wild-eyed in his direction, his mouth still open in surprise.

8

Bolan slid the Weatherby back in its soft case as Buddy Taylor sprinted across the open terrain between his Jeep and the Winnebago, his fat stomach flopping with every step.

The fact that the man was willing to expose himself to more fire from an unknown sniper to reclaim the cocaine, rather than take cover, further confirmed Bolan's belief that Taylor would always play both ends against the middle.

Taylor jumped behind the wheel, spinning the tires in the sand as he headed for the mouth of the canyon.

Bolan knew that the man would flee the ranch if he had any sense at all, but he'd have to pass within a quarter of a mile of the house to get back to the highway. The warrior had no doubt that the man would take the opportunity to trade the Winnebago for one of the faster, less conspicuous vehicles in front of his house.

The Executioner could catch up to him there.

Bolan made his way back to the Land Rover and drove down the hillside, circling into the canyon to the cave's entrance. He stuck his head inside, confirming that the stash had been totally cleared out.

As he knelt to check the chest-shot Colombian, Bolan saw a twitch. He leaned forward and pressed a forefinger against the man's carotid artery.

The pulse was faint.

He squeezed the dying man's face slightly and the eyes opened, glazed over and unblinking against the sun.

"Where did Montoya go?" Bolan asked.

The man coughed, blood from his penetrated lung spewing forward.

"Tell me where Montoya's hiding."

"Coo..." the gunner exhaled softly. "Coo..." With a jerk, he closed his eyes in death.

Bolan rose and walked back to the Land Rover. Coo? It could have been nothing. But then again the Colombian might have been trying to answer. Coo. Colombia? It hadn't sounded that way. Besides, the phone call to the presidential palace that Bolan had forced the captain to make had confirmed that Montoya wasn't expected for several days.

The warrior slid behind the wheel of the Land Rover and pulled through the pass to the road. It was possible that Montoya was still there. The palace could have been ordered to falsely report the general's absence. Montoya might have returned to Bogotá and put out the story, figuring home to be the safest place to ride out the storm.

But somehow Bolan's instincts couldn't buy that. No, Montoya was somewhere else. Somewhere he felt safe— where he could hide until the heat blew over, where he could stay until the Executioner gave up or got killed.

Bolan smiled grimly as he neared Taylor's ranch. He might get killed. That was always a distinct possibility. But the chairman of the board of the cartel didn't know him very well if he thought the Executioner would just get tired and go away.

He parked the Land Rover a quarter mile from the ranch house and scrambled through the rocks and brush.

As he neared the clearing where the house stood, Bolan caught sight of the battered RV parked in front. The expensive rec vehicle had blown a tire, and the tracks behind it indicated Taylor must have limped in on the rim.

Bolan concealed himself behind the stack of firewood on the front porch and looked through the bedroom window. An open suitcase lay on the bed, and from somewhere out of vision, he saw shirts and underwear fly through the air to land in or near the suitcase.

Drawing the Desert Eagle, he crept to the back of the building, eased the screen door open and stepped inside. He heard movement down the hall and made his way silently toward the noise. As Bolan neared the bedroom, he heard labored breathing. Taylor cursed.

Peering around the corner, he saw the merc kneeling in the closet, his back to the hall.

Bolan crept softly until he stood directly behind the man. Taylor was furiously twirling the tumblers of a safe that was dropped into the closet floor.

"Goddamned combination shit . . ." Taylor panted. "Twenty-six left, dammit . . ."

Bolan pressed the muzzle of the .44 into the back of Taylor's neck and reached down, yanking the .45 from the merc's holster. "Go ahead, Taylor," he said. "Open it."

"Pollock? I . . . there's nothing in there. I just—"

"Go ahead. I'd like to see what's inside." Bolan cocked the big automag's hammer, the click sounding thunderous in the small closet. "But you'd better pray there's no gun under the lid."

Taylor spun the combination lock, his shaking fingers failing twice before the door finally opened.

Bolan pressed the Desert Eagle harder into Taylor's spine. "Reach in with two fingers and lift the gun out."

The merc obliged, gingerly setting a Browning .25 auto on the floor next to his knees.

The Executioner swept the gun behind him with a boot. "Now, let's see what else you've got."

Taylor pulled several stacks of paper-wrapped bills from the safe and handed them behind him.

Bolan backed into the living room, shoving the money down the front of his shirt.

The merc turned to face him. "What... There's over a hundred grand there, Pollock. That's my entire savings." The man's eyes narrowed. "You ripping me off?"

The warrior shook his head in disgust. "No, Taylor. Not everybody thinks like you do. I'm helping you pay a debt. Janie Brewer had a sister. But I doubt you knew that. This money goes to her—not that it comes close to evening the score."

Taylor's eyes widened in fear. "Listen, it's not my fault. Those guys held guns on me. They forced me to take them to the dope. I didn't—"

"Save it. I saw the whole thing." Bolan leveled the automag at Taylor's forehead.

"No! Wait!" the merc pleaded. "I've got something you'll want to know."

"Go ahead."

"You haven't talked to Valdez since you got back, have you?" Taylor said quickly. "Let me give it to you fast. Don't shoot me...you're gonna need me." The man's fear-stricken face cracked a nervous grin, and Bolan could see that Taylor thought he had yet another ace up his sleeve.

"Valdez has been a busy little son of a bitch," Taylor told him.

Bolan listened while the guy filled him in on Valdez's plan to reunite with Alpha 66.

And as soon as the double-dealing mercenary mentioned Raul Castillo, the Executioner had his answer as to Montoya's whereabouts.

The words of the dying Colombian. "Coo."

Cuba—only pronounced the Latin way.

Montoya had mentioned Castro in the moments before the Executioner had struck the country inn. Raul Castillo was at the resort working out details for Cuban protection.

It left only one possible answer.

Montoya was probably in Fidel Castro's office right now, planning to saturate the United States with drugs.

"And what were you supposed to get for providing the plane?" Bolan asked. "Somehow, I don't think patriotism was your motive for getting involved."

"Simple. Jackson and—" Taylor paused, a nervous frown replacing the grin. Then he smiled again. "*I* was going to get whatever reward Alpha was willing to pay. That's all."

Bolan thought of the shallow hole Taylor had been filling that morning. "Where's Jackson?" he asked.

"Oh, he left for a few days. Went to . . . Vegas."

"Right. Shall we dig up the hole you were filling this morning and make sure he didn't lose his way."

Taylor blew air from between his lips. "Okay. I killed him, dammit. I had to . . . he wanted the whole reward for himself."

"Uh-huh." The Executioner didn't buy it for a minute. Jackson didn't have the brains or initiative to carry it out. He had been a mindless killer, capable only of following. On the other hand, Taylor might be cowardly and dishonest, but he had proved to be shrewd, as well. The man wasn't stupid.

And that was what made him all the more dangerous.

"Take me with you, Pollock. You need me," Taylor pleaded. "I haven't told you where I'm meeting Valdez, and I won't. I won't lie...I'm scared shitless of you. But I swear to God, there's no way I'll tell you without you killing me—and then you'll never get it."

Bolan mulled it over quickly in his mind. He *could* make Taylor talk, but he didn't have the time.

The Executioner not only didn't know the location of the meeting, he didn't know *when* Valdez would arrive there. But when he did, the little Cuban would find other transportation to Florida if the plane wasn't waiting.

And there was always the possibility that the cartel hit men at the La Paz would track him down. If they got to Valdez first, the Executioner could kiss the plan that had already begun formulating in his mind goodbye.

No, time was of the essence. He had to let Taylor lead him to Valdez and Raul Castillo.

Bolan stepped forward and rested the muzzle of the Desert Eagle on Taylor's forehead. "You take me to Valdez," he said. "But make one false move, do one thing wrong, Taylor, and I'll put one right here." He tapped the barrel on the bridge of the man's nose.

Sweat broke out on the grimy mercenary's forehead. "You got it. No problem. This one's for Uncle Sam."

Bolan didn't honor the statement with an answering comment.

He motioned Taylor toward a chair, picked up the telephone next to the bed and dialed. A moment later a voice answered, "Justice Department."

"Hal Brognola," the Executioner growled.

Bolan kept his eyes and the automag on Taylor while he filled Brognola in on the situation.

"You know we don't have diplomatic relations with Cuba," the Justice man said when he'd finished.

The warrior thought a moment, then said, "Get someone to act as liaison. The Swiss or whoever. We've got to act fast, Hal. I've got to reach Valdez before the Colombians do." He paused. "Or before Alpha gets their hands on Raul Castillo."

"You need Grimaldi?" he asked.

Bolan thought for a moment. They were already working toward countdown. Even if the pilot took off now, it would be several hours before he arrived from Stony Man. He turned toward Taylor. "Where's the Cessna?"

"North a few miles, stashed in an old barn on the flatlands. But, hey, I'm no pilot. I can't fly the damn thing."

"We'll find our own way," Bolan told Brognola and hung up.

He marched Taylor into the front yard toward the Winnebago. "Open the door," he commanded.

The merc fished the keys from his pocket and slid open the panel. Bolan yanked a fragmentation grenade from his combat harness and pulled the pin, gripping the lever firmly.

"What the hell..." Taylor's voice faded away as he ran for cover.

Bolan lobbed the grenade through the door and raced back to the front porch, ducking behind the stacked firewood as the grenade detonated. He raised his head in time to see flaming pieces of brown paper explode out the opening accompanied by gusts of white powder.

"Shit," he heard Taylor call from the corner of the house.

Bolan pushed the merc in the direction of the Land Rover. "Let's go. You're about to start working for your country, all right. Like it or not."

The Executioner started off over the bush to the Land Rover with Buddy Taylor trudging in front of him.

He turned back for a moment as the Winnebago's gas tank exploded, the roaring flames consuming any cocaine that might have survived the grenade.

BOLAN DIPPED THE WING of the Cessna and banked south. He switched the control to auto and leaned back in the seat. From the corner of his eye, he saw Taylor pull a cigarette from the pack in his shirt pocket.

"Don't light it."

"Huh?"

"I said don't light it. I don't intend to spend this flight cramped in here, breathing your smoke."

Taylor laughed and pulled a lighter from his pants.

Without speaking, Bolan reached over and yanked the Camel from Taylor's mouth. He crumbled the cigarette in his hand and dropped the remnants into the ashtray.

Taylor's face reddened, and the angry merc blew air from his lips in disgust. He mumbled unintelligibly under his breath.

They flew on in silence until Taylor turned in his seat. "You know, Pollock, we could be handling this a lot better."

"Is that right?"

"Yeah. Look, this is crazy. Who gives a shit what happens to Castro's best friend? I mean, he *is* the enemy, right?" A grin crossed Taylor's face. Bolan could see the man believed he'd found common ground on which to base whatever argument he was about to pitch.

Bolan sighed. Taylor would never understand that there was no common ground. There never could be between men such as themselves.

"I got a proposal."

The warrior shrugged. "It's a long flight, Taylor. Go ahead."

"Okay. Montoya won't stay in Cuba forever. I mean, he's got an army to run." Taylor waited for an answer. When none came, he continued, "He's bound to think it's all blown over in a few days and go home. You can get him then, right?"

"That's one approach," Bolan agreed. "In fact, it's the one I'd take—if there wasn't a better one."

Taylor turned to face him. "Right. So why don't we grab Raul and just fly him on over to Florida. Valdez has already said he doesn't want the money. We can split it."

Bolan almost laughed. It didn't matter what happened, Buddy Taylor would always be Buddy Taylor. He would see the world, and everyone in it, through the eyes of a man motivated solely by greed. And he would assume that everyone else had the same distorted values that he did.

Bolan shook his head. "I'm not interested in the money."

Taylor threw up his hands. "Okay, shit. I know what you're pissed about. Can't say as I blame you, in a way." He grinned lewdly. "It was pretty good stuff. But damn, Bolan, for what we stand to make, you can buy a hundred little whores like Janie."

The Executioner didn't speak. He turned stony eyes toward Taylor, then returned his gaze to the sky.

That was another thing a man like Taylor would never understand. Taylor's appetites had been his guiding force throughout his life. From the beginning, the crude mercenary had just assumed that the relationship between Bolan and Janie had to be sexual. To him, there could be no other kind.

Well, the Executioner wouldn't waste time or breath trying to explain. Buddy Taylor wasn't worth it.

But the score had to be settled. The books on that account would balance before the Executioner concluded this mission. Taylor was going to pay for the death of a woman whose dying wish had been for a second chance at life.

"Okay," the merc said. "You don't like that, I got a better idea. We don't even need Valdez on this one. We snatch Raul and contact Castro ourselves. *We* run the operation without those government bozos. Can you imagine what that bearded son of a bitch will pay to get his top man back?"

This time, Bolan did laugh. "And you plan to run this show?"

Taylor nodded. "Well, me and you, Pollock."

Bolan turned to stare at the man. Taylor was capable of shifting gears with the speed of a race car. He could threaten vainly one moment, and bootlick with the best of them in the very next. Any angle that might work— that was the one from which he always came. And if it didn't have the desired effect, he changed angles with no more shame than a righteous man kneeling in prayer.

Yeah, he had the speed of a race car, Bolan thought. What he lacked was the precision.

"We could pull it off together with no sweat," Taylor persisted. "Hell, either one of us could handle it *ourselves*."

"And I'm sure you'd try it if I gave you half the chance," Bolan said. "But I don't intend to." He shook his head. "I'd have thought by now you'd have figured out I don't work that way. But from simply a practical point of view, Taylor, you'd be out of your league. Castro would eat you alive."

The merc's face colored again. "I'd beat the hell out of you right now," he growled, "if I could fly this plane myself."

"Yes, I'm sure you would. I've heard your ideas. Now shut up."

Through the Cessna's windshield, Bolan saw the northern tip of the Gulf of California. He checked the instrument panel and set course toward Mazatlán, flying south along the western coast of the rolling blue waves.

Taylor leaned back in the seat, silently chewing the end of an unlighted cigarette. Bolan could see the wrinkles in his forehead as he squinted in concentration.

The man was scheming again. On what new twist, Bolan didn't know. He was angry that he'd lost the cocaine and the money it would have brought. Now, he was even losing the reward Alpha 66 would have paid for the delivery of Raul Castillo.

Buddy Taylor was both greedy *and* angry, and the combination could mean only one thing: the Executioner's problems with the double-dealing merc weren't over. They couldn't be until he'd pointed out the meeting place with Valdez. Then perhaps, the Executioner could rid himself of this fat albatross once and for all.

Taylor broke the silence as they neared Mazatlán. "Okay, shit, never mind. I've had enough of this crap anyway. All I want now is out. I'll take you to Valdez, and then there's a sweet little thing in Mazatlán I think I'll go throw a leg over. And good riddance to *you*, Pollock."

"Wrong."

"Huh?"

"I said, 'wrong,' Taylor. I'm not taking my eyes off you until I've got Montoya."

"Hell. All I want's a piece of ass. You can't hold that against me, can you?"

"You stay with me."

Bolan reached under the pilot's seat and located one of the false panels where the cocaine had been hidden. He slid it open and removed the Beretta and Desert Eagle, dropping them into the compartment. He turned to Taylor. "Touch them," he said flatly, "and I'll kill you."

"Hey, no sweat. I just want this thing over."

The Executioner turned back to the controls and began the descent. In the distance, the tower advertising AeroMexico and Mexicana Airlines popped over the horizon and then the runway appeared below.

The Executioner kept one eye on the runway as they touched down. He kept the other on his reluctant companion.

9

The Mexican customs officer swaggered toward the Cessna as Bolan and Taylor leaned against the door. He stopped in front of the plane and wrote on the clipboard in his hand. *"Turista?"* he asked Bolan.

"Yes," Bolan replied in Spanish. "We're only here for the afternoon."

The Mexican nodded and walked slowly around the plane, jotting more entries on the visitor's pass. He turned back to Bolan. "Do you have the plane registration?"

Bolan smiled. "Somewhere. I'm an unorganized man. It would take some time to find it."

The customs man nodded. "There's no reason to inconvenience our American friends. It's obvious you're good men, seeking only a little rest and relaxation, no?" he looked from Taylor's scuffed and scarred combat boots to his face. "Perhaps you have another form of identification you could show me before you go on your way to enjoy the delights of our fair city?" he smiled in anticipation.

Bolan produced several bills and handed them over.

The money disappeared into the Mexican's back pocket. "Have a pleasant stay," he said, and turned away.

The Executioner climbed back aboard and opened the panel beneath the seat. He slid the Beretta and Desert Eagle under his shirt before rejoining Taylor.

"Handled like a champ," the merc said, grinning.

Bolan ignored him as they walked toward the terminal. He didn't like bribing officials—of any country. But in Mexico, it was a way of life. The police, from *federales* on down, were underpaid by the government and accepting "tips" for minor infractions was expected as part of their income. It was the officer's own interpretation of what constituted *minor* that led to the problems within that system.

Bolan saw the uniformed man again as they cut through the terminal. He left Taylor at a row of vending machines and walked up to the man.

"Excuse me."

The Mexican turned to him, frowning. "Yes?"

"I'm worried about the safety of my plane," Bolan said.

The Mexican official's chest puffed in importance. "You Americans. You're not the only people with security for—" He broke off in midspeech at the sight of the hundred-dollar-bill in Bolan's hand.

"I would like you to make sure no one comes near the Cessna."

The official snatched the bill. "I will guard it with my life." He turned briefly to where Taylor was uncapping a Coke bottle. "Is your friend included in this restriction?"

"My *friend* is especially included."

The customs official headed for the Cessna.

Bolan and Taylor continued toward the front of the terminal, where Bolan knew he'd find a line of cabs. They took seats in the back of a crumbling, unmarked

Ford and listened to the cabbie's endless prattle as they rode to the Mazatlán harbor.

The warrior ordered the cabdriver over to the curb at a shopping center a half block from their destination.

"Look," Taylor said as they got out, "you can handle it from here. It's a Hatteras 48—should be easy enough to spot. I think I'll look up the hooker I mentioned. You keep the plane. I'll find my own way back."

Bolan shoved him toward a phone booth outside a souvenir shop. "Bad idea," he said. "I want you where I can see you."

Bolan dropped a coin and dialed a special number that rang Brognola's private line at Justice. A few minutes later, the big Fed came on the line.

"The Swiss embassy here is handling it," the Justice man said. "Castro's agreed to the trade. But he wants it on his terms."

"What a surprise."

"Yeah. It's got to go down in Cuba, Striker. It was the only way he'd negotiate. You up for it?"

"Tell me where and when," Bolan replied.

"They're still working out the details. Castro doesn't know that we don't even have Raul, yet. We're stalling through the Swiss as much as possible, but there's a time element involved. If he doesn't get his buddy back quick, he's threatened to tell the press that the CIA kidnapped him." Brognola took a breath. "That wouldn't help us much on the world scene."

"Politics are somebody else's department. You worry about that. I'll get Raul. Where do I go from here?"

"Naval Air Facility, Key West," Brognola instructed. "Don't announce your approach—we don't want to risk Alpha 66 or anyone else picking up your air waves."

"What *about* Alpha?" Bolan asked. "Do they know anything?"

"I don't know, Striker. But to make sure, we've asked the Company boys to keep a close rein on them the next few days."

"Be sure they do," Bolan said. "They'd shoot their own mothers for a chance at Raul."

The warrior hung up, and he and Taylor started toward the docks. They passed fishing and pleasure craft and then the lines of a Hatteras 48 became visible in the distance. Valdez was on deck with a mop.

The little Cuban looked up as Bolan stepped on board. He smiled quickly at his visitor, then a frown spread slowly across his features. He looked at Taylor, then back at Bolan. "Why are *you* here?" he asked, dropping the mop.

Bolan looked him square in the eyes. "I've come for Raul."

Valdez shook his head, his hand dropping to the hilt of his Bowie knife. "I am sorry, Señor Pollock. I have admired your skill and courage since the beginning. But you cannot have him. He must pay for his crimes against my people."

"And he will. Someday. But right now there are more important things to consider, Valdez, and I don't have time to line them up for you." Bolan pushed past the little Cuban and started for the ladder.

Bolan heard the swish as the Bowie left the leather sheath. He ducked instinctively as the massive blade cut an arc over his head, the rays of the hot tropical sun reflecting off the wide blade as it passed above him.

The Executioner turned as Valdez slashed again, returning the wide blade in a vicious, backhand cut. Bolan shuffled backward toward the ladder, the Bowie flashing less than an inch from his throat.

The warrior's hand moved toward the guns in his belt, then stopped. The thunder of the Desert Eagle would bring harbor officials running from all directions. The suppressed Beretta would be quiet, but already they had attracted the eyes of passengers on nearby vessels.

A knife fight in southern Mexico wasn't uncommon and merited only the sporting interest of the crowd. But the restrictions on firearms were rigid, and the sight of a gun, particularly with a suppressor attached, would likely mean the notification of police.

Bolan stepped to the side as the little Cuban lunged, the knife snagging in his shirt as it passed his ribs. He threw a short jab, and Valdez's head snapped backward, dragging him across the deck.

"Just drop it," Bolan ordered. "I don't want to hurt you."

The Executioner didn't want to kill the little Cuban. Like Janie, he was basically a good person gone wrong. Regardless of how misdirected he might be, his primary goal was to rid his homeland of the bearded tyrant who had reigned for the past three decades.

Unlike Buddy Taylor and men of his ilk, there was still hope for Valdez.

Bolan retreated once more as Valdez leaped forward with a downward, overhand slash toward the skull. Anticipating the next move, the warrior reached out and caught the little Cuban's wrist as it started up in an underhand, disemboweling stroke.

A hard right cross sent Valdez crumpling to the deck, unconscious, while the Bowie knife bounced off a seat cushion then settled next to him.

Bolan kicked the weapon aside and turned to Taylor. "Watch him. I'm going below to get Raul."

Castillo lay on the bed in the main stateroom, bound and gagged. His eyes widened as Bolan bent to cross the threshold.

"Perhaps there is a God, after all," the Cuban gasped when Bolan removed the gag. He laughed, tears forming in the corners of his eyes. "But more likely, Fidel is still able to manipulate the Americans at will." He rubbed his wrists as soon as Bolan freed him from his bonds. The smile left his face as he assumed command. "We must leave for Cuba immediately."

"No, not immediately."

"I said *immediately*," Castillo snarled. "You must be of some importance for Fidel to have chosen you. But I'm the defense minister. *I* will take charge now."

Bolan drew the huge .44 Magnum from beneath his shirt and shoved it under the Cuban's nose. "You're badly mistaken," he said. "Now get up."

"What? You didn't come at Fidel's orders?"

"Hardly." Bolan pushed Castillo up the ladder. "Try to break for it when you reach the top," he said, "and I'll put one between your shoulder blades." He shoved the Desert Eagle into the man's spine for emphasis.

The Executioner followed the Cuban up the steps, returning the .44 to his belt as he reached the top. As the warrior stepped out into the sunshine, he saw Felipe Valdez laying on the deck.

But he wasn't simply unconscious. The little Cuban's throat had been sliced from ear to ear, the blood-covered Bowie next to his body.

Buddy Taylor was no where to be seen.

Bolan shoved the minister into a seat and ran to the bow, scanning the docks. Taylor was sprinting back toward the boat, his red face threatening to explode from exertion.

"I...couldn't...catch them," the puffing man gasped out.

Bolan didn't answer.

"There . . . were three . . . of them," Taylor continued between breaths. "Cubans, I think. Snuck up on me."

The Executioner scanned the area again. The people on the nearby boats were conducting business as usual—the same people who had been so interested in the knife fight minutes before. Surely the sight of three men coming aboard the Hatteras and cutting the throat of an unconscious man would have sparked their curiosity once more.

And from the stateroom, only a few feet below deck, Bolan had heard no commotion.

No, three men hadn't boarded the boat, overpowered Taylor and cut Valdez's throat. *One* man had knelt quietly out of sight and killed the unconscious Cuban.

Then he'd taken off down the dock and waited until Bolan and Castillo came above, sprinting back with another of his ridiculous, implausible lies.

Bolan stared into Buddy Taylor's eyes. The cowardly mercenary was now responsible for the deaths of all three of his Vampire Bats. The world had a score to settle with this miserable excuse for a human being, a score that would be settled by the Executioner.

But it would have to wait. Far in the distance, Bolan saw two harbor policemen hurrying along the docks, revolvers drawn. Someone *had* alerted authorities, either concerning the earlier knife fight or the murder immediately afterward.

It didn't matter which reason now brought the law racing down the harbor. Bolan didn't need their circumspection under any conditions.

"Take Valdez below," he ordered Taylor, then turned to Raul Castillo.

"I don't have time to explain the whole situation right now," he said, "but I'll hit the high spots. You're going to walk out of here next to me, and you're not going to open your mouth until I tell you to. If you do, I'll kill you." He patted the bulges beneath his shirt. "You understand?"

The Cuban nodded as Taylor reappeared from below.

Bolan looked at him, his eyes narrowing. "Let's go."

The warrior placed Castillo between himself and Taylor, and they walked quickly away from the Hatteras and the oncoming police. They followed the docks to the end, then turned away from the sea toward the phone booth Bolan had used earlier.

The Executioner cast a final glance over his shoulder as the two Mexican harbor police stepped onto the Hatteras's deck.

The Executioner hailed a cab and motioned the minister in after Taylor, taking the seat on the Cuban's other side. "Airport," he told the driver.

Bolan saw one of the harbor police appear from the docks behind them as they pulled out into traffic. The police had discovered Valdez's body, and they were now looking for the murderer. If he was lucky, they'd figure it for just another of the many robbery-killings by local thugs that went unpublicized by the Mexican Bureau of Tourism. But if the police suspected the involvement of foreigners, they were likely to encounter problems at the airport.

Bolan leaned over the seat and pressed several bills into the driver's hand. "We're in a hurry."

The driver grinned and nodded his head. He floored the accelerator, cutting in and out of the honking cars around him.

At the airport, Bolan paid off the cabbie and hurried Castillo toward the Cessna. Taylor followed, a cat-who-ate-the-canary grin on his face.

The same uniformed customs officer they'd dealt with earlier stood next to the Cessna. He smiled graciously as the three men approached the plane. "You're leaving so soon?"

Bolan nodded.

"Ah, and you've picked up a friend, I see," the Mexican said. A greedy expression covered his face as he turned to Castillo. "Your passport, please," he said.

"He's lost his passport," Bolan explained, handing several hundred dollar bills to the official.

"Many thanks. And visit us again—" he looked at the bills in his hand "—Señor Benjamin Franklin." He threw back his head in laughter as he walked away.

Several minutes later Bolan taxied toward the runway as Buddy Taylor tied the Cuban's hands and feet. It didn't make sense. Why had Taylor killed Valdez? The shifty merc's sole motivation had always been greed, and cutting Valdez's throat wouldn't make him a penny.

No, killing Valdez hadn't been Taylor's objective. It had been simply a means to some other end.

Taylor had been looking for an excuse to slip away from Bolan's watchful eye ever since they'd left the ranch. But to do what?

The plane lifted off the ground as several police cars screeched to a halt in front of the terminal. As Bolan dipped the wing and headed east toward Florida, he could make out the tiny form of the customs officer pointing through the air toward the Cessna.

BOLAN KEPT the Cessna low over the desert, flying under the radar line until he neared the Sierra Madre Occidental.

He doubted that police in Mazatlán had gone to the extent of alerting the Mexican Air Force. If they were spotted, it would likely be entered into the logbooks as just another of the countless, unidentified aircraft that were common to the Mexican skies.

Probably. But there was no sense taking chances at this stage of the game.

The Cessna rose as they reached the sharp peaks, and Bolan guided the plane through passes and valleys to further confuse any electronic eyes that might be watching.

Bolan switched the Cessna to automatic pilot as they left the mountains and turned to Taylor. "Get Raul up here where I can talk to him," he ordered.

"Why?"

Bolan turned to face the merc, and Taylor rose from his seat, mumbling under his breath.

"We'll be landing in Florida," Bolan told the Cuban moments later. He saw a mask of fear come over the man's face.

"So. You wanted only to collect the reward yourself," he taunted. "It's *you* who will turn me over to the terrorists."

"It's an idea," Bolan said. "But no. You'll be going home. I'll be escorting you there in a trade arranged with your premier."

Castillo's eyes showed both surprise and relief. "And who is so important to you that you will trade me for him?" he asked.

"A friend of yours. Juan Montoya."

The Cuban smiled. "Yes, I see. But he's not a friend. Merely a business associate." He paused. "And he's a fool. You're getting the bad end of this trade, I think."

Bolan shrugged. "Depends on your point of view. Just don't convince me you're right." He glanced out the window. "It's a long way down."

"Where will we be landing once we reach Florida?" he asked.

"You know all you need to know," Bolan replied. "Taylor, take him back to his seat."

Bolan kept the plane on autopilot until they neared the peaks of the eastern Sierra Madres. Having seen no sign of pursuit so far, he ascended to a comfortable altitude over the mountains and returned the Cessna to automatic.

Taylor moved to the seat across from him. "Listen," he whispered. "We gotta talk."

Bolan was sick of the man. "There's nothing left to talk about."

"Yeah, there is. What happens to me when this is over?"

Bolan didn't bother to reply.

"That's what I thought," Taylor said. He looked briefly behind him at Raul. "Look, I got a plan."

"I'm not surprised."

"Well, this one you're gonna like," Taylor continued. "We—"

Bolan shook his head. "Forget it. I'm tired of your ideas. Keep your mouth shut for the rest of the flight."

Taylor slunk back to the seat across from the Cuban.

"Perhaps you should hear him out," Castillo remarked. "Perhaps his idea has some merit."

Bolan kept his eyes ahead, ignoring the man.

"Perhaps it's the same idea that I have." The Cuban minister waited for the response, which didn't come. "Fly me directly to Havana," he finally said. "You'll be welcomed with open arms and have riches beyond your wildest dreams."

"I've been through all this with Taylor, pal. Before you stepped onstage. I'm not interested."

The warrior turned back to the steering column, periodically glancing up at the mirror. Taylor and Raul continued whispering to each other at the back of the cabin.

They flew on across the mountains until the deep blue of the Gulf of Mexico appeared in the distance. Taylor finally made his way back to the cockpit and took the seat across from Bolan. "You were right," the merc said. "We've talked enough." His hand dropped to his combat boot and he pulled a single-action .22 Magnum minirevolver from inside his sock. "Compliments of Valdez." He leaned forward and pressed the tiny gun into Bolan's ear. "I'll take charge from here."

"How far do you think you'll get without a pilot?" the warrior asked.

"Oh, yeah," Taylor said. "I *did* tell you I couldn't fly, didn't I?" He snickered. "This'll surprise the hell out of you, Pollock, but I *lied*."

Castillo stood up at the back of the cockpit and shuffled forward, smiling. "It seems you have been outsmarted, señor." He turned to Taylor and extended his hands. "And now, if you please, amigo."

"Not yet," Taylor said.

From the corner of his eye, Bolan saw the Cuban flush. "What do you mean?" he demanded.

Taylor turned to him, the gun still trained on Bolan. "Sit down," he ordered.

Castillo dropped to the seat behind Bolan.

"I gave you your chance, Pollock," Taylor spit. "You and your damned God-country-and-flag crap. Think you're better than everybody else, don't you?" He waited for an answer. "Don't you?" he taunted.

Bolan remained silent.

"What are you doing?" the Cuban asked.

"Sorting things out." Taylor laughed. "You're still in first place, greaseball. I suspect Fidel will be able to pay more than these Alpha sons of bitches. But I'm not selling myself short this time. I'll be taking bids for your ass, so to speak. Free enterprise, you know. It's the American way." Taylor broke into hysterical laughter once more.

Bolan turned slowly toward him. "You have any idea what will happen if one of those rounds hits the wrong part of this plane?" he asked.

"Oh, for chrissakes," Taylor said. "Give me a little credit, will you? I mean, I know I'm not the big shot expert on everything that you are, but I'm smart enough to know that the odds are way against that happening. Besides, professional hazards and all that."

Bolan watched the white-capped waves of the Gulf through the Cessna's window. The strategic planning mode of the Executioner's brain went into effect as he considered his options.

Taylor wasn't likely to shoot him where he sat. The Cessna was still on autopilot, but the commotion a dying man could create could knock the system askew in several different ways. The merc would then have a difficult time getting Bolan's body out of the way so he could get behind the steering column and take control before the Cessna went down. And if the first shot didn't kill, the fight that the cowardly merc had to know would take place could easily send the plane crashing into the Gulf.

All three of them would die. And if Bolan had learned anything at all about the treacherous parasite who sat next to him, it was that Buddy Taylor didn't want to die.

Bolan's hand moved slowly toward the controls on the instrument panel. If he could gain control of the plane he might have a chance of knocking Taylor off balance.

He'd been inching his hand toward the autopilot control when Castillo's bound feet flew up in the air and hit Taylor's extended arm at the wrist, forcing the cocked minigun past Bolan's head.

The .22 Magnum sounded as loud as the Desert Eagle in the small cockpit as the round sailed harmlessly through the roof of the Cessna. Bolan turned toward Taylor as the Cuban dived forward, his head butting the surprised merc in the chest and sending him sprawling over the steering column.

Taylor's elbow crashed into the automatic pilot button on the yoke.

All three men lurched forward against the instrument panel as the Cessna nose-dived toward the water below. Bolan pushed hard, fighting to put enough room between his chest and the steering column to maneuver the controls. Jerking his head against the downward pull, he thrust backward with every ounce of the strength in his shoulders and arms and pulled back on the grips.

The Cessna swooped ten feet from the waves and leveled out across the water.

As Taylor regained his balance, he swung the gun back toward Bolan. The Executioner wrapped his hand over Taylor's, trapping the minigun between both of their fingers.

The Executioner felt the heat and heard Taylor scream as the .22 Magnum barked again, the round sailing down into the seat by Bolan's thigh.

Blood streamed from the merc's fingers as he fought to pull his hand from the Executioner's grip.

Castillo dived forward again, raised an elbow and attempted to hook it over Taylor's neck in a headlock. The Cuban's hands, still bound close to his body, forced his arm to a halt across Taylor's eyes.

Blinded, Taylor screamed again, throwing himself and Castillo backward to the rear of the cockpit. The weight of the two men at the tail threw the Cessna's nose upward and forced Bolan back against the seat. The plane rocketed skyward, the engine coughing and threatening to stall.

The Executioner reached up and grasped the steering mechanism. He pushed forward as the Cuban and Taylor, still entwined, came pummeling to the front once more. The two men rebounded off the instrument panel and fell against the clamshell door on the passenger's side as the Cessna's wings rocked right and left. Someone's knee bumped the safety latch as both men went to the floor.

Bolan fought to keep the aircraft from going into a lateral spin as the combatants struggled near the door. He saw Castillo's bound feet kick out and down, and the bottom half of the clamshell door swung open in the slipstream.

The warrior bore down as the additional drag banked the Cessna down and to the left. Glancing sideways, he noticed that Castillo had disentangled his arm from the bleeding mercenary and was pushing him toward the opening.

Bolan righted the Cessna. The inertia from the sudden jerk as the plane resumed a horizontal position worked with the Cuban, pushing Taylor closer to the door.

With a loud groan, Castillo suddenly thrust both legs across the floor, catching Taylor squarely in the chest. The aging merc slid through the door and disappeared with a bloodcurdling scream.

The door slammed closed once more.

10

Bolan felt the wheels hit the runway and slowed the airplane to a halt. Two jeeps tore across the tarmac, and in the back of the lead vehicle sat a tall, broad-shouldered man whose U.S. Navy uniform displayed the rank of captain.

Bolan helped Raul Castillo out of the plane and cut the ropes from his hands and feet as the jeep came to a stop a few feet away.

The officer stepped down to the ground, glanced quickly at the Cuban without speaking and extended his right hand to Bolan. "Mr. Pollock?" he asked. "Welcome to NAF, Key West. I'm Captain George Hronopulos."

Bolan took the firm grip and felt the calluses. The base commander's face was deeply creased and tanned. Here was one officer who did more than shuffle papers. Bolan stared the big Greek in the eye and found that Hronopulos didn't flinch. With receding brown hair and a slight paunch starting just over his belt, George Hronopulos looked like an aging Hercules.

"We'll proceed directly to DESDIV headquarters for briefing," Hronopulos said. He shot Raul Castillo another glance and turned back to the jeep.

Bolan and the Cuban took seats in the second vehicle next to the driver and another man. The Executioner looked at their uniforms. The driver wore dungaree bell bottoms and a blue chambray shirt. The two stripe "crow" on his left sleeve indicated his second-class Navy rate. The name tag sewed over his left breast pocket said, Addington. The khaki uniform and anchors on the shirt collar of the man in the back seat marked him as a chief petty officer.

For the most part, they looked no different than the many other sailors who were coming into view as they neared the long row of buildings in the distance. But little things gave them away and distinguished them from the others.

Bolan saw the butt of a Smith & Wesson Navy Model .22 extending from a custom-made cross-draw holster on the driver's belt. The holster was too long for the weapon—unless a silencer had been threaded onto the barrel.

The Executioner glanced over his shoulder to the chief petty officer. Pressed between his knees was a Stoner M63A1 machine gun—a weapon used exclusively by Naval SOF teams.

Both men had discarded standard Navy headgear. The driver had tied a camouflage sweatband over his brows while the man in the khakis wore a floppy jungle hat.

"SEAL Team 6?" Bolan asked the driver, knowing the answer before he got it.

Addington looked up in surprise and nodded. He jerked his head forward, indicating the captain's jeep that had already parked in front of one of the buildings. "Down this morning from Norfolk. The skipper hasn't briefed *us* yet, either."

Bolan smiled. The U.S. Navy SEALS were as good as they came, and SEAL Team 6 was the best of the best.

They were specially trained for counterterrorist operations and would provide far better security than the average shore patrolmen on temporary security duty.

But their presence indicated something else as well. Unless Bolan's positive first impression of George Hronopulos was wrong and the man was a raving paranoid, the captain was expecting trouble from some quarter.

Addington pulled in behind the lead jeep and the two SEALS escorted Bolan and Castillo to a steel door. The man in the sweatband punched numbers into the combination lock, and the door buzzed open, revealing a long, brightly lighted passageway.

They stopped for another lock at the first door on the left before the two SEALS took the Cuban down the hall. Bolan saw the emblem embossed on the glass in the door: an ancient Greek griffin, his lion's body rampant below the snarling head of an eagle, spread his wings in flight while a submarine broke in half between his hind claws.

Bolan entered the room and took a seat across from Hronopulos, who sat in the middle of a semicircle of folding chairs. They were soon joined by the two SEALS and four more hard-looking young men in cammies.

When everyone was seated, Hronopulos looked at Bolan. "I don't know who you are, Pollock, but you've got some clout somewhere. As soon as you're briefed, you're in charge." He paused, his heavy eyebrows lowering as he studied the newcomer. "Normally I'd fight like hell to oversee an op like this myself. I don't just turn my base over to everyone who walks through the door—and to hell with what the fat asses in Washington say." Deep furrows appeared on the big Greek's forehead as he continued. "But I'm big on gut-level reactions, and the one I get from you is that you're the man for the job.

"Anyway," Hronopulos went on, "the exchange is scheduled for tomorrow evening. You'll shove off on the *M. E. Hart* in the morning."

Bolan frowned. "That means we've got security problems, Captain. You're aware of the Alpha 66 involvement. Any reason we can't set sail right now?"

Hronopulos nodded. "Yeah. The same Washington sand crabs I just mentioned have decided that this is too good an opportunity to let slide by. They've got an intelligence-gathering team on their way down now to rig the ship with all the latest electronic James Bond crap. I don't go for it, either, Pollock. It means we've got approximately fifteen hours to baby-sit our friend."

The Executioner exhaled deeply. "This is an open base. Access is easy. Where do you plan for us to hole up until morning?"

Hronopulos shook his head in disgust. "You won't like this, either. Seems Washington's handling this with kid gloves. They don't want our friend here in cuffs and chains, and they don't want him locked up. It's been strongly suggested that I extend the use of my quarters and make him feel at home."

"You're right," Bolan said. "I don't like it. And as far as the delay goes, I thought Castro was in a hurry to get his buddy back."

"He was. But he agreed to wait until tomorrow night." Hronopulos rubbed a big hand across his heavy beard. "Probably gives the bearded wonder time to let Russian spooks set up their own surveillance." The captain motioned towards the SEALS. "I haven't always been a pencil pusher, Pollock. Until a year ago, I was with Naval Special Warfare Group 2. Helped form SEAL Team 6 back in '80.'' He paused a moment, and Bolan could tell his mind was drifting back to an assignment with which he'd been more at ease. "I've kept security light to avoid unwanted attention, but the men I've got here are the best. I ought to know—I trained them. They're at your disposal.''

Bolan turned to the six men. "You'll help me provide security until after the exchange," he said. "The main threat while we're still on land is Alpha 66. We don't know that they're even aware we've got Raul, but it pays to prepare for the worst rather than hope for the best.'' Bolan hesitated, then continued. "The way I see it, the weak length in the chain is the next fifteen hours. We've got an open base and a bureaucratic chain of command that doesn't understand the risks diplomacy implies in a situation like this. Primarily that's because they've never been in situations like this themselves.

"When we get to sea," the warrior went on, "the primary enemy becomes Castro himself." He turned back to Hronopulos. "Have the details of the exchange been worked out?''

Hronopulos shuffled his feet uncomfortably. "Yeah. Castro wants to meet in the hills overlooking Bahiá de Nipe. That's his old stomping grounds, the area where he grew up. He's agreed to two escorts—you can pick whoever you want." He indicated the SEALS. "But if he sees more than three faces, he'll consider it a trap and start shooting. If you ask me, the old man's half-convinced the whole thing's another CIA plot to take him out. Castro's promised to bring only two bodyguards, himself. And Montoya. And if anyone believes that, I've got some beachfront property for sale in the everglades.''

"We won't disappoint him," Bolan said. "And we don't need another escort. I'll take Raul in myself."

The SEALS looked disappointed. Addington peered at him from under the sweatband. "But sir—" he started.

Bolan shook his head. "Two men won't be any better than one. Not under these circumstances. There's no point in risking another life when we don't need to."

"Which brings me to the question I've been wanting to ask," Hronopulos said. "Pardon my ignorance, but what in hell makes you think Castro will ever let you off the island alive once he has his pal, here?"

Bolan smiled grimly. "You were with NSW 2, Captain. Their home is an RAF base in western Scotland, isn't it?"

Hronopulos nodded. "Mull of Kintyre. Mobile Mine Assembly Group 2's there, too. What are you driving at?"

"I understand they store some interesting equipment there. I think one of their special 'backpacks' might be just the insurance policy I'm looking for."

The captain grinned. "I see where you're heading, Pollock, and it just might work. But you realize, if you'll pardon the pun, this could damn sure blow up in your face."

"Right. How long will it take you to get one here?"

Hronopulos frowned. "That depends. If we go through channels, I'd say we'll have it by the turn of the century." He blew air between his lips in disgust. "But if we can sidestep the bureaucratic bullshit, it won't take long. I'll get them started now." He picked up the phone. "Get me Lieutenant Oven, RAF Machrihanish, Becky," he said. "Ring me back as soon as he's on the line." He hung up.

"We'll leave Raul here for the time being," Bolan told him. "He's as safe here as anywhere." He turned back to the SEAL team. "Which one of you's the demo man?"

A short, compact man with coal-black hair looked up. "Gunner's Mate Second-Class Patrick Harkin, sir," he said. "Underwater and ground demolition."

"You picked up on what the captain and I were talking about?"

The young man grinned. "I did, sir."

Bolan stood up. "Let's go. We'll have to wait for delivery from Scotland before we make the final preps, but there's plenty we can do in the meantime."

Harkin rose and followed Bolan to the door.

The captain walked them down the hall and outside into the blistering Florida sun. "It's the Alpha aspect of this thing that worries me," he confided. "I know the Company boys are supposed to be keeping watch over their little Cuban pals, but this is like training an attack dog not to eat dry dog food until he gets the command, then dangling a sirloin steak in his face. The temptation's too great."

"I'm not crazy about the setup myself," Bolan admitted. "But there's not much we can do about it at this stage of the game. We'll just have to make the best of the situation."

George Hronopulos extended his hand once more. "You know what I think I hate most about all this, Pollock?" he asked.

Bolan gripped the big Greek's hand.

Hronopulos looked back at the building where Raul Castillo was under temporary guard. "Eating dinner with the son of a bitch tonight." He shook his head. "And in my own goddamn house."

HRONOPULOS USHERED Raul Castillo, the six Navy SEALS and Bolan into the front hall of his house and left them in the hands of the Cuban maid.

"Show them to their rooms, will you, Serifina?" he said. He couldn't resist a grin when the woman stared at Castillo. She knew who he was, and she looked as if she'd love to tear out his eyes with her fingernails.

Hronopulos walked down the hall to the den and grabbed a bottle of ouzo from the shelf behind the bar. He poured two fingers into a highball glass, hesitated a moment, then replaced the bottle. No, it wouldn't pay to get sloshed tonight. Not with that fuzz-faced son of a bitch's minister of defense as a houseguest.

Hronopulos took a seat in an overstuffed leather armchair and thought again about the mysterious man who had brought in Castillo. He didn't buy the Pollock name. It didn't fit, somehow—not that it was that unusual for government agents to go under aliases.

But George Hronopulos wasn't even sure Pollock— or whatever the hell his name really was—*was* a government agent. At least not the traditional kind. Oh, he was working *with* the U.S., all right, but he certainly didn't fit the mold of the gray pin-striped spooks in the Riviera sunglasses. Rance Pollock acted more like a Special Forces soldier.

The big Greek glanced at his watch. Oven's plane should touch down soon. Hronopulos thought of what the man would be bringing from the base in Scotland, and he shuddered.

No, Pollock definitely wasn't CIA. He'd known countless Company men during the past twenty-five years, but he'd never met a spook yet who'd have balls big enough to try what Pollock had planned.

Hronopulos crossed his legs and felt the belly flesh strain against his belt. He frowned. Soft, dammit. Well, that's what happened when a man was put out to pasture. It didn't seem to matter how much time he spent in the base gym or out on the track. It wasn't the same as running twelve miles with a sixty-pound rucksack and weapons.

And, dammit, it wasn't as much . . . fun.

Hronopulos stood up as the maid escorted Pollock, the Cuban and two of the SEALS into the den. He held up his glass. "Drink?" he asked. The Americans shook their heads. The captain glanced at the untouched ouzo in his hand and set it on the bar.

"Cuba libre," Castillo said, "if you have it."

Hronopulos looked down at the shorter man. Free Cuba, my ass. "I've got it," he said.

He walked behind the bar and poured two shots of Myers's rum into a glass. Opening the small refrigerator, he found a half-empty bottle of Pepsi with no cap. Hronopulos smiled to himself when it didn't fizz as he stirred it into the rum.

Rather than hand the glass to the Cuban, he set it on the bar and turned to Bolan. "Where's the rest of the team?"

"I've got them set up around the perimeter," the big man said. "These two will join them as rovers in a few minutes."

The men sat down to await dinner. Hronopulos smiled to himself. With the exception of Castillo, they looked about as comfortable as nuns at a male strip show. The Cuban was making himself right at home, relaxing on the couch and sipping daintily at his flat drink like some Dade County faggot.

But the rest were men of action. All of them. They had no business baby-sitting this commie bastard, himself included.

The maid returned to announce dinner, and the two SEALS disappeared to join the others. Hronopulos followed Bolan down the hall, noting the slight bulge under his sport coat next to the shoulder blade.

The big man walked next to Castillo. He hadn't let the Cuban out of his sight since they'd left DESDIV headquarters. He'd even insisted on sharing a room in the house with him.

George Hronopulos followed the men to the room his wife called the conservatory. The entire back wall was a series of jalousie windows that opened onto the patio. In the evenings, the windows stayed open, the gentle breezes off the Straits of Florida blowing through to rustle the leaves of the potted palm trees and cool the room.

Gleaming silver utensils and china for four stretched the length of the long, glass dining table. Hronopulos saw that his wife was already seated, and he looked her over. She wore a long, black cocktail dress and pearls, and dammit, she still looked good after almost thirty years as a Navy wife.

But he couldn't help the small amount of resentment that always hit him whenever he saw her, now. Mary had talked him into accepting this assignment. She'd finally convinced him he was getting older; it was time to take it easy. But Mary had adapted much better than he had to the social functions and other bullshit no real sailor could ever stomach.

The three men joined the lady as a steward in whites served the salad. Hronopulos and Bolan ate in silence while Mary and Castillo began chatting like old friends.

"I have always wished to visit Cuba," Mary said.

"Well," Raul replied, smiling, "perhaps that can be arranged after I inform my premier of the excellent treatment I have received in your home." He paused and looked around in mock fear. "Unless, of course, the next course is . . . liver."

Mary giggled like a schoolgirl.

Hronopulos stuck a forkful of salad in his mouth and washed it down with a sip of the white wine the steward had just poured. He noticed Bolan hadn't touched his glass.

"It's a privilege to have you," Mary said.

Hronopulos bit down on his fork.

The steward returned with a silver tray and circled the room, setting bowls in front of the guests and their hosts. He was ladling soup into Castillo's bowl when suddenly the ladle dropped from his hand and splashed into the bowl.

"For God's sake, *do* be more careful, Dizon," Mary chided in embarrassment.

The steward stood motionless for a moment, his eyes widening, then he slumped to the floor, a trickle of blood dripping from the corner of his mouth.

Bolan dived toward the Cuban and pulled him to the floor, jerking a huge automatic pistol from under his coat as they fell. The sounds of machine-gun fire erupted at the front of the house.

Hronopulos grabbed his wife and fell over her as Bolan rose and started for the windows. "Get them upstairs," the warrior ordered.

Crawling along the tile of the floor, Hronopulos pushed his wife and Castillo in front of him. When they were through the door, they stood and hurried down the hall and up the stairs. The Cuban's mouth was hanging open in shock; the bronze skin of his face had turned a sickly gray.

In the master bedroom, Hronopulos shoved the two into the closet before jerking open the top drawer of the dresser and jamming a Government Model .45 down the front of his trousers. From under the bed, he pulled a Carl Gustav M-45B submachine gun, rammed a full magazine home and bolted a round into the chamber before setting up in front of the closed closet door.

He was as mad as hell at Mary for getting him into this "retirement" job in the first place, and he hated the pretentious little prick who now cowered in the closet with her. He'd be more than happy to put a round between the bastard's eyes himself under the right circumstances.

But he'd be damned if anybody else was going to do it, and no one, by God, was going to hurt his wife.

Not in George Hronopulos's own godamned house.

BOLAN CRASHED through the jalousie windows, his arms crossed to protect his face. The constant staccato of automatic fire came from the front of the house, but the bullets sailing through the jalousie windows had been silenced. Whoever was behind the long-range weapon somewhere to the rear had fitted it with a suppressor.

The Executioner sprinted across the patio and onto the lawn as dirt and grass flew by his feet from the silent rounds. He hit the ground running and rolled behind the trunk of a stout elm tree at the rear of the yard.

He'd noted the angle of trajectory of the tiny hole that appeared in the wall behind the steward. The Sheetrock had rippled downward slightly, below where the bullet had entered, which meant the sniper was firing from high ground.

Bolan surveyed the immediate area. At least one of the SEALS should have been at the back. He stuck his face around the elm and scanned upward. He jerked back as a thud hit the trunk.

The captain's home sat at the edge of the housing area. Directly behind the yard grew a small cluster of trees and broad-leaved plants that separated the area from a row of training facilities in the distance. Bolan stuck his head around the tree once more.

Nothing. They hadn't come for him. Whoever had fired through the open windows of Hronopulos's house had one goal in mind—kill Raul Castillo.

Bolan straightened and sprinted through the trees, watching his flanks with peripheral vision. As he neared the edge, he could see through the leaves to the training buildings.

On the far side of the sonar calibration facility, he saw a man in jeans and a T-shirt jump from the roof as a Ford van screeched to a halt. The side panel opened and arms reached through to grab the rifle before pulling the man inside. The van sped away.

So much for open bases, Bolan thought.

He slowed to a jog until he reached the one-story building. Close to where the man had jumped, he found a pile of packing crates and, holstering the big .44, climbed to the roof.

Bolan walked to the edge facing the back of the captain's house. In the sun-softened tar by the edge of the building he could make out knee prints, and empty brass .308 casings lay scattered around the area.

Bolan dropped to the ground and jogged back to the house where the chief petty officer was setting Pat

Harkin onto the couch in the living room. Blood was dripping from the young man's leg.

Harkin grinned up at Bolan through gritted teeth. "Caught one in the calf, sir. Carelessness on my part. Sorry."

George Hronopulos came down the staircase followed closely by his wife and the Cuban. The big Greek had the sling of an M-45B around his neck and looked as if he were itching to put it to use. "You see who it was?" he asked Bolan.

The warrior shook his head. "Never got close enough." He turned to where the officer sat, applying a field bandage to Harkin's leg. "You?"

Both men shook their heads. "There were a dozen or so, though," Harkin said. He winced as the officer tightened the bandage. "Wearing street clothes. I was close enough to tell you this—they all had dark hair and skin—so I guess we can take a pretty good guess, huh? And I got the definite feeling they weren't really trying to kill anyone. More of a diversionary tactic."

Bolan nodded. "It was to draw attention away from the rear. Who was supposed to be out back? I didn't see anyone when I ran through."

Harkin's brow lowered. "Addington, I think."

One by one, three more SEALS returned to the house.

"Anyone seen Addington?" Bolan asked them.

All three shook their heads.

Bolan left two of the men at the house and took a third, carrying an MP-5, to the backyard with him. "Reed, you check to the right," he ordered the man.

The Executioner had gone only ten paces into the clump of trees when he spotted the camouflage field boot sticking out of the brush. He called to his companion.

The warrior tore away the leaves and vines to reveal the body of the short, wiry man. The silenced .22 had fallen from the cross-draw holster and lay next to the M-16 still clutched in his hands.

The bullet had entered just above the ear on the left side of Addington's head, piercing the camouflage sweatband and taking half of the young SEAL's head with it as it exited on the other side.

"Harkin was right about the fire in front being a diversion," Bolan told Reed as the man stared down at the corpse of his fallen comrade. "It was the part about not trying to kill anybody he was wrong about."

Bolan and Reed carried Addington back to the house.

"All right, dammit," Hronopulos thundered when he saw the body. "I've had enough of this bureaucratic, ass-kissing bullshit to last a lifetime." He jammed a thumb at the Cuban, who sat passively in an armchair. "This son of a bitch is going to the ship, and I don't give a rat's ass what the sand crabs in Washington have to say about it." He stalked to the phone, the instrument jerking each time he jammed a heavy finger into a number. "This is Hronopulos. Get me Brow Watch."

The big Greek barked orders to both stations, and then turned to Bolan. "There'll be shore patrolmen when we reach the ship, and I've got half the Marine detachment on their way here, now." He paused. "That sound okay to you, Pollock?"

Bolan nodded and turned to Castillo. "Stand up." The Executioner turned toward Harkin. "Can you walk?" he asked.

Harkin rose unsteadily, took two cautious steps, then limped to Bolan. "Yes, sir."

Bolan directed him to stand next to the Cuban. The Executioner eyed the two men. "Close enough," he said, then turned to Mary Hronopulos. "Have you got a wig?"

"Well, yes. I have a fall," she replied, looking puzzled.

"Would you get it?" Bolan asked.

"We'll need two transport vehicles," the warrior said to the captain. "I want one of them to look civilian."

"We can use Mary's Seville," Hronopulos offered. He lifted the receiver and dialed another number.

"How long before we can expect the Marines?" Bolan asked.

Hronopulos shrugged, the phone wedged between his shoulder and cheek. "Ten, fifteen minutes."

The blood was returning to Mary Hronopulos's face. She turned toward her husband. "Should we... finish dinner while we wait?"

Hronopulos's eyes shot daggers at her from across the room.

Bolan looked at Mary and said, "Get the fall, please, Mrs. Hronopulos." He glanced back to Harkin. "And some dark makeup. We'll find plenty to keep us occupied between now and the time they arrive."

Mary Hronopulos turned and disappeared up the stairs.

Bolan turned to Castillo. "Take off your clothes."

"What?"

"Do it."

The Executioner turned to Harkin, but the grinning SEAL was already unbuttoning his shirt.

11

Bolan helped the Marine slip the soft body armor over Raul Castillo's head. He fastened the Velcro closures and dropped the steel plate in the pocket over the Cuban's heart.

Castillo began buttoning the shirt that Harkin had removed moments before. "This is heavy," he complained.

"Tough shit," Hronopulos growled from the background. "If it was up to me you wouldn't be wearing it."

The phone rang, and Hronopulos grabbed it. "Yeah?" He pressed the instrument to his ear and gritted his teeth as he listened. "I don't give a damn, Featherstone," he finally shouted. "I've lost one man already 'cause you spooks can't control your little friends. I stand to lose more, not to mention showing my ass all over the national press as the station commander who couldn't even get his man to the ship." He paused, listened, then yelled again. "You're damn right we'll discuss it tomorrow morning. That is, if any of us are left. And that includes you, Featherstone. 'Cause I promise you this. If I make it through the night, I intend to kick me some CIA ass before I do any *talking*."

He slammed down the receiver and turned to Bolan. "The spooks felt them out yesterday, and the Alpha 66 honchos didn't even know Raul was here. But they've got some renegade splinter group, or whatever you want to call it, and they're *damn* sure aware of it. Word has it that they got a phone call from somebody yesterday afternoon."

Bolan nodded. Buddy Taylor was dead, but he was throwing monkey wrenches from beyond the grave. Bolan remembered the phone booth at the Mazatlán harbor where he'd called Brognola. The timing was just about right. Taylor had had plenty of time to kill Valdez and sprint to the booth while the Executioner had been below with the Cuban.

Valdez had died simply to cover the unscrupulous mercenary's last double cross.

"How many troops in this splinter group?" Bolan asked.

Hronopulos shrugged. "There's no way to tell. But Alpha 66 numbers in the thousands."

Bolan frowned. "What they're calling a splinter could turn out to be a log."

He watched as Reed finished applying Mary Hronopulos's dark foundation makeup to Harkin's face. The stocky SEAL looked foolish in the patchy beard the Executioner had cut from the woman's fall. It would never pass close inspection.

But Bolan didn't plan on this stray faction of Alpha 66 getting a good look. Wearing Castillo's clothes, Harkin would make a convincing Cuban from a distance.

The warrior gathered the men around him. "All right," he began. "Harkin will ride decoy with the Marine escort. I'll take Raul in Mrs. Hronopulos's Cadillac." He turned to Reed and the chief petty officer. "The chief and Reed ride with me."

Hronopulos stepped forward. "Like hell. You go with the Marines, Chief." He faced Bolan. "You're in command, Pollock. I can't overrule you, and I wouldn't if I could. But it *is* my base and I feel a certain responsibility for..." He jammed a thick index finger toward Castillo and looked at Bolan expectantly.

The Executioner stared into Hronopulos's eyes. Bolan could tell that not only did the man want to be in on the action, he *needed* to be.

He nodded to Hronopulos. The big Greek had already proved he was a good man under fire. He was a commander, but he hadn't hesitated to follow Bolan's orders so far. That was a quality most men of his rank lost somewhere during their climb up the military ladder—the ability to obey as well as issue orders.

Bolan led his team to the garage and slid behind the wheel of the Cadillac Seville. He waited as Reed took the shotgun seat and Hronopulos put Castillo on the floor in the back, covering him with his legs.

"This is...humiliating," the Cuban complained.

The Executioner barely suppressed a smile as he heard a thump, then a soft groan come from the back seat.

"Excuse me," Hronopulos apologized. "Me and my big feet." His voice didn't sound too sorry.

Bolan watched through the garage-door window as the Marine-Navy convoy pulled away from the house. He'd give them a two-minute lead.

The Executioner had refused the offer of an armed car to ride shotgun on the circuitous route he'd charted to the pier. That would have defeated the purpose. If this plan worked—and there were never any guarantees—it would be because they slipped to the ship without drawing attention.

He threw the Seville into Reverse and backed into the driveway. The street behind him was deserted. So far, so good.

The warrior drove slowly, keeping the Caddie under the twenty-mile-per-hour residential-area limit as they moved through the long row of officers' homes. Then, tapping his foot lightly on the accelerator, he jumped the car to thirty as they drove through the base maintenance area.

The Executioner frowned, not happy with the way the engine choked when he'd accelerated. He hadn't expected Mary Hronopulos's car to be a high-performance racing machine, but it hadn't entered his mind that the vehicle might break down on the way to the ship.

Bolan made a right-hand turn, heading away from the dock for several blocks before taking a street parallel to the route the convoy had followed. With any luck at all, the decoy would keep Alpha 66 safely away from Castillo. But as they neared the dock area, the margin of safety would have to be narrowed. Bolan would bring the vehicle in from the opposite direction, but the closer they got to the ship, the closer the Caddie would get to the convoy.

They crossed the base maintenance area and passed the Acey-Ducey and Seaman's clubs. Bolan glanced at Reed in the seat next to him. The black man's eyes darted left to right, scanning both the ground and the rooftops as they drove. In the rearview mirror, Bolan could see Hronopulos doing the same.

As they turned left and started the last leg to the water, the Executioner spotted a battered Chevy parked halfway down the block. Smoke rose from the open hood, and two figures in dresses and scarves stood next to the vehicle, apparently waiting for help.

Apparently was the operative word. Bolan felt the muscles in his chest tighten. He wasn't sure why, but it didn't look right. "Get ready," he told the other two.

Reed drew back the bolt of his silenced MP-5, and Bolan saw a flicker in the mirror as Hronopulos raised the Gustav M-45B.

Bolan drew the Desert Eagle and held it in his left hand as they neared the parked vehicle. They were twenty yards from the car when the two "women" turned to face them. Both had beards, and both held MAC-10 machine pistols.

The Executioner reached through the open window and rested the big .44 on the Caddie's hood, tapped the trigger and dropped the closer gunner. The man's dress flapped up over his hairy knees as he hit the ground.

The warrior floored the accelerator, but the engine sputtered and coughed. The Seville slowed.

"Dammit, Mary," he heard Hronopulos mutter under his breath as the first burst of gunfire from the second gunner trashed the Seville's windshield. Reed slumped against Bolan, his face and chest riddled with holes.

The warrior eased up on the pedal and the Caddie sprang back to life. He held it halfway to the floor, and the big car gradually gained speed as they passed the scarfed gunman.

They chugged past the Chevy as more rounds exploded around them. Bolan saw Hronopulos twist to face the rear, his right knee pressed against the back of the car seat. Strapping his leg down with the seat belt, the big Greek leaned out the window and fired the M-45B.

The scarfed man returned fire. Two rounds hit Hronopulos in the right forearm, and the Gustav fell to the street. Without hesitation, Hronopulos's left hand drew the .45 from his belt and continued firing.

The enemy gunner went down, but his final round hit a rear tire. The Seville jerked hard to the left. Hronopulos was thrown up against the roof by the sudden momentum. He flopped back away from the car as they fishtailed down the street.

The Executioner brought the Caddie under control and limped in on the rim to the alley behind the Naval Exchange. He grabbed Reed's silenced MP-5 and ripped the canvas magazine belt from the strap around his neck.

Hronopulos exited the vehicle, pulling Castillo out after him with his bloody arm.

In the street in front of the building, they heard the screech of tires. Bolan and Hronopulos each grabbed an arm and dragged the Cuban down the alley. Two blocks away they stopped behind the bowling alley and dropped to concealment behind a row of Dumpsters.

Bolan looked at the captain. The strain was beginning to show. The big Greek's face had turned bright crimson, and his chest heaved under labored breathing as he squatted in the semidarkness. Blood poured from his wounded arm, but he held the .45 steady in his other hand, muzzle up and ready.

Bolan tore the chambray shirt from Castillo's back, exposing the dark blue body armor. He wrapped the cloth around Hronopulos's arm, tying it tightly, then twisted the knot.

They heard footsteps down the alley as hushed voices conversed in Spanish.

"What now?" Hronopulos panted.

"The backup plan," Bolan replied.

Hronopulos grunted. "Didn't know we had one."

"We always do. Fight."

The big Greek chuckled.

The Executioner squinted through the darkness. The footsteps were drawing near, and he could make out movement as shadowy figures searched the alley a block away. "How much farther to the ship?" he asked Hronopulos.

"Six blocks."

"We'll have to make it on foot," Bolan told him. "Grab an arm."

They dragged the Cuban to his feet and moved out cautiously, putting as much distance as possible between them and the renegade members of Alpha 66. When they hit the cross street, Bolan scanned the area before the three men sprinted under the streetlight and back to the darkness of the alley on the other side.

The warrior shoved Castillo behind another Dumpster as shots rang out from somewhere across base.

"Sounds like the decoy worked," Hronopulos grunted.

Bolan nodded and jerked a thumb back down the alley where the searching figures had reappeared. "Tell *them*. Let's go."

At the next intersection, they ducked behind a parked panel truck as a carload of men raced past, the barrels of automatic weapons poking out through the open windows. Bolan waited until they were out of sight, then pulled the Cuban across the street.

They continued moving silently in the shadows, crossing the next two streets without incident. The salty smell of seawater drifted to them, and Bolan could see the destroyer in the distance.

But a two-block stretch of open grass field separated them from the pier.

The autofire was closer now, and escalating. Bolan turned to Hronopulos. The big Greek was holding his own, but the blood vessels in his face and neck threatened to explode each time his chest heaved outward. "It's open country from here on in," the Executioner said. "You up to it?"

Hronopulos nodded. "Goddammit, I'm a... SEAL...Pollock," he wheezed. "At least I used to be. And we can do any damn thing we *want*...to do."

Bolan hoped so.

They took off at a job across the field, Castillo stretched between them. At the far end of the dock, Bolan saw sporadic muzzle-flashes as automatic weapons blazed in the darkness.

Suddenly they were framed in light as two cars rounded a corner and jumped the curb to the field in pursuit. Dirt and grass flew into the air as rounds ripped into the ground by their running feet.

Castillo broke away from their grasp and turned, frozen like a startled deer in the headlights. There was a break in the fire, then a lone shot rang out and the Cuban screamed, collapsing onto his back on the ground.

Bolan laid down cover fire with the silenced MP-5, the weapon sending barely audible *phutts* through the open field. He reached down and grabbed Castillo by the front of his body armor. He turned toward the ship, towing the shocked man by the vest.

Hronopulos fell in behind, wheezing for air and losing ground with every step.

Bolan dropped the silenced MP-5 and snatched the big .44 Magnum from his side. The time for silence and stealth was over. What they needed now was the attention of some of the Marines who were still battling the Alpha troops at the other end of the docks.

The warrior fired four rounds over his shoulder as he ran, the Desert Eagle thundering out its cannon booms. Castillo tripped and fell to the ground once more. The Executioner whirled and dropped to one knee, emptying the magazine into one of the oncoming vehicles and taking out a headlight.

He looked over his shoulder. They were still a hundred yards from the ship, but a U.S. Marine Corps jeep was racing toward them from the other end of the quayside. He shoved a fresh mag up the butt of the .44.

The men in the two vehicles ceased fire, then turned their guns on the approaching Marines.

Hronopulos puffed to a halt by the Executioner's side. He looked past them to the ship. "Better...let me go first. They'll recognize me. They're liable...to shoot you . . . in all the confusion."

"Take off," Bolan said. "We'll follow." He turned and emptied another magazine of .44s at the enemy cars, then grabbed the Cuban again and scrambled after Hronopulos.

Scattered shots still rang over their heads as they neared the ship. Bolan watched Hronopulos lumber up the forward bow, the career sailor flashing automatic salutes at the stern and OD on the run. In front of him, the Executioner heard the watch system ring eight bells and then the 1MC boomed "NAF, Key West, arriving," over the gunfire.

Bolan dragged Castillo up the bow and shoved him onto the quarterdeck. He undogged the hatch and pushed the Cuban through as a round careened off the steel plating over his head. The Executioner turned and dropped the lone gunman, then ducked through the hatch into the superstructure.

Hronopulos lay exhausted on the deck of the passageway.

The ship's skipper slid down the ladder railing from the bridge, staring at Hronopulos as the big Greek's chest heaved. A wry grin spread across the man's face as he came to attention in an exaggerated salute to his red-faced colleague. "Nice of you to drop in, George," he said. "Not a bad job you did out there... for such an old fart, that is."

Hronopulos raised his arm and saluted the skipper— his middle finger extended as it touched his forehead. "Up...yours...Haz," he panted and grinned.

The skipper turned to Bolan and offered his hand. "Captain Hasbrook Edwards. Welcome aboard the *M. E. Hart*."

Bolan took his grip. "Are the electronic intelligence specialists finished setting up?" he asked.

"No, but they're on board. And your... *order* from Scotland just arrived. Lieutenant Oven brought it on board a half hour ago."

"Good," Bolan said. "The electronics people can finish while we sail."

"Fair enough," Edwards walked to the bulkhead and flipped a toggle switch on the ship's communication system. "This is the captain," he said. "Pass the word. Make all preparations for getting underway." He turned back to Bolan. "Anything I can provide for you gentlemen?"

Hronopulos's laugh echoed throughout the superstructure. "Yeah," the big Greek replied, his breath still coming in puffs. "Get our little friend some dry diapers, will you, Haz?"

Bolan and Edwards turned to Castillo who lay on the deck across from Hronopulos. A dark, wet stain covered his crotch.

12

Bolan and Hronopulos followed Captain Edwards through the destroyer's passageways. Edwards stopped at a stateroom door, opened the lock and they stepped inside. He flipped another switch on the ship's communication system and barked orders into the microphone. A few minutes later, a steward appeared.

Edwards indicated Castillo with a jerk of his head. "Bring this man food, and a clean shirt and dungarees. Then have dinner for five sent to my at-sea cabin." The skipper leaned back into the radio. "Send down a signalman," he told the bridge.

Bolan felt the deck roll beneath his feet as the destroyer got underway. Through the lone porthole, he saw the water around the ship begin to churn, white bubbles sparkling in the dock lights.

Hronopulos opened the hatch and the signalman entered the room, saluting.

"I want you to stay with this man, Flags," Edwards ordered. "Officially he's not a prisoner, but I don't want him leaving this room until I give the word. Understood?"

The signalman nodded. "Aye, aye, sir."

Two men were waiting outside in the passageway when they reached the captain's at-sea cabin. Edwards began the introductions as they crossed the threshold.

"Lieutenant Jesse Oven," he said, nodding toward a thin, wiry man in camouflage fatigues and a floppy jungle hat. "One of George's original SEALS."

Bolan grasped his hand.

"And this is the head of the intelligence crew," the skipper continued. "Delmar Buvinger, Direct Support Detachment. Grab a seat, gentlemen. You both know George." Edwards slid into the chair behind his desk. "This is Rance Pollock. Don't know for sure who he's with—but he's in charge."

Bolan and Oven took seats on the folding couch-berth while Buvinger sat down in the small armchair across from them.

Edwards pulled a manila file folder from a desk drawer, crossed his legs and rested it on his lap. "I've been in touch with the Justice Department," he said, looking at Bolan. He opened the folder and pulled a pair of half glasses from his breast pocket. "Brognola, I think his name was...yeah. Anyway, here's the low-down so far. Fidel Castro has agreed to exchange Juan Montoya for his minister of defense at 1900 tomorrow. A Cuban soldier will meet Raul and no more than two guards—he was adamant about that—on the beach at Bahía de Nipe."

Bolan saw the skipper squint through the glasses at the open folder. "I've got the coordinates here, and there's supposed to be a small pier. Anyway, Castro's coming himself and he'll only have two men, too."

"Bullshit," Hronopulos bellowed.

"Probably," Bolan agreed. "But it doesn't matter. I'll take Raul in myself."

"Castro's also stipulated that the ship remain in international waters. Not that I was too excited about getting closer anyway," Edwards said. "This is a touchy situation, Pollock. It could blow up in our faces at any time. How do you plan to go ashore?"

Oven looked at Bolan. "We can use a Zodiac, if you want," he said. "But it's slow."

Bolan thought a moment. The Zodiac *was* slow, and there was always the chance of the rubber dinghy capsizing during the six-mile journey. Castillo's behavior under pressure so far had been far from heroic. Bolan didn't even know if the Cuban could swim, and the thought of splashing around in the waters of the Caribbean trying to save a screaming man didn't appeal to him.

Bolan shook his head. "We'll take your gig, Captain. It'll be safer and faster than a Zodiac. It'll mean more than two men accompanying Raul, but only to the pier. The crew won't need to leave the boat."

Edwards nodded. "I'll notify the crew."

Hronopulos turned to Bolan, the big Greek's eyes narrowing. "Let me ask you just one question, Pollock. Once you're on the island, you're in Castro's ballpark. I know what you're planning. And like I said, I like it. But Fidel-baby isn't playing with a full seabag. In short, what if it doesn't work?"

Buvinger spoke for the first time. "Excuse me. I don't know what you gentlemen are referring to, but I think I can put your fears to rest, Captain."

Bolan looked a him. Buvinger wore thick glasses under the bushy white eyebrows that were the only hair on his head. His eyes darted nervously as he scanned the cabin every few seconds. "We'll be using long-range surveillance equipment to monitor your activities, Mr. Pollock," he said. "Both audio and visual. It's to ensure your safety as well as secure proof if Castro reneges on his promises. And there's always a chance we may pick up some stray intelligence that could be useful later." Buvinger paused, his thin chest expanding as he drew a deep breath. "It's the best equipment available, but we can't rule out failure due to unforeseen circumstances. I'd like you to wear a recorder and body mike as a backup precaution."

Bolan thought a moment. Trusting electronic surveillance to protect him from whatever double cross Castro might have in mind was an exercise in futility. No matter how fast the men on the ship picked up danger signals, they could never reach the island in time to be of any help.

Once the Executioner hit the beach, he'd be on his own.

That was why Bolan had taken his own precautions. And he would already be loaded down without dragging along recorders and bugs.

Still, it made sense to record an exchange that had the potential to escalate into a global incident. "What type of recorder are we talking about?" he asked Buvinger. "Nagra?"

"Yes. And a relatively small Fargo body transmitter," the intelligence expert answered as if reading his mind.

"Fine," Bolan said. He was familiar with both items. The reel-to-reel Nagra wasn't much bigger than a pack of cigarettes, and the Fargo transmitter was even smaller. There would be plenty of room left for his own "insurance policy."

A knock sounded on the cabin door. Edwards opened it and allowed the steward to enter. The skipper motioned him toward the desk, and the white-jacketed man set down a tray of steel-covered plates and left.

"Anybody hungry?" Edwards asked.

"Let's finish first," Bolan said. "Then we'll eat. I'll take Raul and meet whoever Castro sends—"

Oven interrupted. "Let me make a suggestion. You *know* Castro's not coming to meet us with just two troops. Now, I know you've said you'll take Raul in by yourself, and it's easy enough to figure out why. But dammit, I'm a professional, too. It's as much my job as yours. That's why they sent for me." He glanced briefly at Hronopulos. "Even with me along, you'll probably be outnumbered twenty to one. But two guns are always better than one, and who knows when that extra gun might just make the difference."

Bolan looked him up and down. He was a SEAL, and he had to be good or they'd have shipped him out somewhere long ago. The Executioner would have his hands full looking after Castillo and trying to second-guess the Cuban premier. It wouldn't hurt to have someone watching his back.

"Suit yourself," he told Oven. "We'll follow our contact wherever—"

Suddenly the door burst open and the skipper's runner sprinted into the room.

"What the hell?" Edwards demanded.

"I just came from the stateroom, sir," the runner panted as his hand flashed to his forehead in salute. "The prisoner is missing, sir." He paused to catch his breath. "And Flags is dead."

BOLAN RUSHED down the passageway with the other two men at his heels. Not bothering to wait for the captain's key, he hit the door with his shoulder. The lock sprang, and the Executioner burst into the stateroom, the Desert Eagle clenched in his fist.

The signalman lay sprawled on his side, his open eyes staring fixedly across the room. A thin line of blood trickled from just above his left ear to the deck.

Bolan threw open the door to the head and looked inside.

Nothing.

The food Edwards had ordered sent to the stateroom sat untouched on the desk. Bolan lifted the steel cover, and steam rose from a bowl of boiled potatoes.

"They can't have gone far," Bolan said. He turned to Edwards. "Who was the steward?"

Edwards shrugged. "There's close to three hundred and fifty men on board this ship," he said. "I don't know them all."

The captain's runner looked up. "New man, sir," he said. "Transferred on board this afternoon. Filipino, I think. At least his name indicated it."

Bolan shoved the Desert Eagle back in his hip holster. "Call the watch and issue a security alert," he told Edwards. "We'll check the boats first. If we don't find them there, we'll work backward."

Edwards flipped the switch on the communications system as Bolan, Oven and Hronopulos raced through the door, down the passageway and climbed the ladder to the bridge. They sprinted through the superstructure hatch and out to the weather deck on the ship's starboard side.

"How about the rubber dinghies?" Bolan asked Hronopulos as they sprinted along the side of the ship. He glanced at the drum-shaped objects attached below.

"They'll be locked up," the big Greek puffed. "A steward wouldn't have access."

Bolan ran to the captain's gig and stepped on board. The cabin was empty.

That left only one possibility. Unless the steward and Castillo were hiding somewhere on the destroyer rather than attempting immediate escape, they had to be in the motor whaleboat.

Bolan looked at Oven as several sailors, bearing .45s and Remington 870s, raced out of the superstructure and took up security positions on deck.

"Check the fan rooms and any other place that might be unlocked," he told the SEAL. Oven sprinted away across the deck. Bolan turned to Hronopulos. "Where's the whaleboat located?"

"Port side," the big Greek replied.

Bolan glanced at the superstructure. "Can we get through?"

Hronopulos shook his head. "Be faster to circle."

The Executioner raced along the deck as waves swelled over the rails of the *M. E. Hart*. Hronopulos struggled to keep pace as they rounded the bow of the destroyer and headed toward the whaleboat. Bolan could hear clanging sounds as the small craft descended the side toward the water. He peered over the rail and saw the top of Castillo's head.

The steward stood next to him, a silenced Colt Woodsman .22 in his hand.

"Can you stop it?" Bolan yelled at Hronopulos as the big Greek joined him.

Hronopulos didn't answer. He chugged past the Executioner to the davits. Bolan heard the shrill screech of metal on metal as the whaleboat came to a halt thirty feet below.

Two sets of eyes looked up to the rail. Then the steward threw an arm over Castillo's head and pulled him close. He pressed the barrel of the Woodsman into the man's neck.

A salty mist of seawater splashed him in the face as the Executioner drew his own suppressed weapon from shoulder leather. He wiped the moisture from his eyes with a shirtsleeve.

"¡Alto!" the man with the gun screamed. "¡Por la Cuba libre!" His eyes darted from the whaler's bow to stern, frantically seeking escape from the boat that hung suspended, halfway to the sea.

Bolan moved slowly, extending his arm over the rail and sighting down the barrel of the Beretta. "Drop the weapon," he ordered.

"No!" the man below shrieked. "The bastard is my prisoner. He goes to my comrades to pay for his crimes." He hugged Castillo to his body and jammed the .22 deeper into the flesh of the man's neck.

The warrior clung to the rail with his left hand as a wave rolled into the ship. He closed his eyes as more mist sprayed his face.

Water dripped from Bolan's nose to his shirt as he opened his eyes once more. He stared through the moonlight at the men below. The Alpha 66 kidnapper's body was hidden behind Castillo's. The only area of exposure was the upper right quarter of the man's face.

"Drop your gun!" the Alpha man demanded. "Or I will kill him here!"

Bolan hung on as another wave rocked the ship. His timing had to be perfect. He'd have to time the waves, then wait until the ship steadied and fire in the split second before another wave spoiled his aim.

And hope the ocean stayed out of his face.

"This is your final warning!" the man below screamed into the wind.

"No," Bolan replied. "It's yours. Throw the gun over the side."

Hronopulos joined him at the rail. "Mexican stand-off?" he asked.

"Cuban," Bolan said grimly. He squinted into the dark sights of the 93-R.

The Executioner waited until the ship crested the next wave.

He squeezed the trigger.

The suppressed Beretta coughed discreetly in his hand. Bolan felt the 9 mm recoil shoot up his wrist as a sudden spray of salt water blinded him.

He wiped his eyes and looked below.

The Alpha 66 gunman lay on his back in the motor whaler, a blood-filled cavity where his right eye had been.

Hronopulos engaged the davits, and the whaler rose to the deck. Bolan pulled Castillo back aboard the ship. The Cuban said nothing as they entered the superstructure and descended the ladder to the stateroom.

Edwards met them at the door where a sailor was already busy, repairing the lock Bolan had broken.

"I'll call the watch," the skipper said. "We'll get security to stand by the rest of the way."

Bolan shook his head. "Don't bother." He pushed Castillo past the repairman and followed him through the open door.

Turning back to Edwards and Hronopulos, he closed the door behind him.

JUAN MONTOYA FELT a trickle of sweat roll from his forehead to the lapel of his white linen suit. He rubbed the damp palms of his hands across his pant legs. As if they had a mind of their own, Montoya's feet shuffled nervously on the floor. The Colombian general pushed hard on his thighs to make them stop.

Reaching into the side pocket of his sport coat, Montoya located a vial and popped two antianxiety tablets into his mouth.

For the past two days, ever since the incidents at the country inn and airport, Juan Montoya had been riding an emotional roller coaster. His moods swung from fear to anger to sorrow and back to fear. With time for a reasonable amount of lust thrown in between, Montoya thought. He glanced again at the red-haired Cuban secretary.

The buxom woman swiveled to face him in her desk chair, the white crotch of her cotton panties flashing past his eyes as she crossed one nylon-covered leg over the other. "I am sorry, General Montoya," she said, smiling. "It shouldn't be much longer."

Montoya shrugged. His heart rose in his chest as his mind lingered on the image of her shapely legs.

He warned himself not to think of her. Women had always been his Achilles' heel.

The lust in Montoya's heart was replaced by a sudden surge of hatred. Particularly women with red hair.

And the last one had almost killed him.

Montoya tried to force his thoughts from Janie, but she refused to leave his mind. Then the hatred gave way to an overpowering melancholy. She had been special. She had been everything he had ever dreamed of possessing in a woman.

But she had betrayed him.

Montoya turned back to the woman behind the desk. Her flaming hair caressed her cheeks as it fell to her shoulders, looking almost orange against the smooth brown of her face and neck. The hair was obviously dyed—or rinsed—as women liked to say. Montoya wondered if the red of Janie's hair had been the true color. Perhaps she had deceived him even more than he knew, dying her pubic region, as well.

Forget her, he almost said out loud as the anger returned. It was over. The redheaded witch received what she deserved for her treachery.

Montoya ran his hand along the tattered upholstery of the couch. Everywhere he looked since arriving in Cuba, he saw signs of the economic depression that plagued the island.

He thought of his own country where poverty, if not vanquished, had at least been restricted to a few select barrios of the major cities. At least it couldn't be seen, as it could throughout the streets of Havana.

Montoya felt the pride of accomplishment flow through his veins. He smiled.

And who has brought this booming economy to Colombia? he asked himself.

The pride swelled higher in his breast.

No, not the government. A king.

King Cocaine.

Montoya thought of a Carlos Lehder, Pablo Escobar, and the early days of the cartel. It had all been so easy. American customs had been lax, and the weekend flights from Lehder's island in the Bahamas had shown profits far beyond anything any of them had imagined.

They had all become rich. And the money had financed his political campaigns as he rose nearly to the top of the Colombian government.

Montoya jerked involuntarily as a wave of anxiety hit his chest. Was it over?

The entire operation had gradually become more complicated as the American attitude changed. What had been called the drug problem became the drug war. Then suddenly the American armed forces were being used and the cartel had been forced to ally itself with that madman, Manuel Noriega. Then even the Panamanian general had fallen to the outraged Americans.

Montoya lighted a cigar and stared at the closed office door. Fidel Castro was a definite improvement, even if he was a rude and ill-mannered boor. The bearded dictator had made an initial mistake by putting that clown, General Ocha, in charge of the cartel shipments. And Ocha had drawn attention.

But now that Raul would be the liaison to Colombia, things should run more smoothly.

Montoya glanced impatiently at the diamond-studded Rolex on his wrist as anger replaced anxiety. He had been treated well since his arrival, but there was no excuse to be kept waiting like this. He was top general of a country far more prosperous than this dying island.

As if Castro had read his mind, the phone on the secretary's desk suddenly buzzed.

"His Excellency will see you now," the woman announced. She stood, running her hands down the front of her skirt to smooth the wrinkles. Her high heels clicked across the tile to the door as Montoya followed, his eyes glued to the curves of her buttocks as they rolled beneath the confines of the tight fabric.

He crossed the threshold and saw the old man behind the desk. Suddenly the realization that he was at the mercy of the most feared dictator in the Western world nullified all the emotions that had yo-yoed through him since his escape at the airport.

It didn't matter that he was the commander-in-chief of the Colombian armed forces. It didn't matter that Cuba was slowly dying. He glanced at the picture of the Cuban premier and Nikita Khrushchev on the wall behind the desk.

Fidel Castro was still alive and functioning. He wielded far more political power in the world arena than any Colombian ever had or would.

And Juan Montoya's fate lay in his hands.

THE MAN with the gray-streaked beard coughed twice and felt the pain burn through his upper chest. From the breast pocket of his faded green fatigue shirt, he produced a handkerchief and spit phlegm into the coarse white linen.

He leaned back in the chair and studied a framed photograph on the wall above his deck. A younger man, smiling, the beard still black above the olive-green shirt, shook hands with an overweight, balding, Slavic-looking man.

Nikita. Sometimes he missed the loudmouthed old braggart.

Fidel Castro glanced at the picture once more. In the background, just above where he and Khrushchev linked hands, was the proud face of his best friend.

Castro turned his eyes to the bottom drawer on the desk's left side. He coughed again and longed for one of the large cigars locked away behind the cold metal. How long had it been since the doctors had found the tumor? How long since he'd been forced to give up one of the last true pleasures he had? Almost three years now. And not a moment in one of those long, grueling days had passed in which he wouldn't have traded anything he owned for another of the dark-leaved Cuban masterpieces.

Redirecting his gaze to the photograph, he examined the beard and wondered when the gray had first appeared. He couldn't remember. He had been far too busy in the early days to pay attention to such trivial, personal details.

He had held a vision.

The old man smiled, recalling the naive enthusiasm that had driven all of them to restore his native land, an overpowering, all-encompassing drive that sometimes seemed to have a life of its own. He had held a vision that he could rebuild Cuba far past the affluence it had enjoyed under the imperialistic domination of the devil, Batista, and that someday he would see the decadent Americans overthrown and a world governed by the working people.

That had been more than thirty years ago.

The vision had never taken shape.

Castro felt the sharp pain in his back as he tried to rise from the chair. He put his hands on the desktop and let his arms assist his legs as he rose to his feet. He crossed the room to the window overlooking the streets of Havana and gazed upon the consequences of his failure. Ragged, hungry children roamed the streets while their equally impoverished mothers searched the trash containers for food.

Yes, he had failed. The pain in his chest forced another uncontrollable series of spasmodic coughs. Would he live to see that failure reversed?

The U.S. embargo had hurt the island far more than he was willing to admit. It was the Americans he had to thank for the poverty that was slowly destroying his country. He glanced across the street to the market area where a pudgy, red-faced tourist with a camera slung around his neck bargained with one of the street merchants. A woman, equally fat and sunburned, looked on.

Castro shook his head. In desperation he had finally opened the island's gates to American tourism, and thousands had poured into the country. But they had no appreciable effect on the economy. As always, the capitalists took more than they gave.

And now they had taken his one true friend.

Raul had been his sole confidant since Che Guevara's death, and Raul was certainly the only one who could be trusted with the delicate liaison between Cuba and the Medellín cartel. That relationship had almost been exposed before it had gotten off the ground. It had even become necessary to throw General Ocha to the wolves.

The old man laughed as he thought of Raul at the trial, pointing his own guilty finger at the accused. The popular general's arrest and public disgrace had served two purposes. It had eliminated the only serious competition Raul had to become the next premier, and Cuba had shown the world that they, too, were combating narcotics.

Castro snorted. Ocha had been a pawn. A scapegoat. To his dying day, the old fool would never figure out what had happened.

Now, the cartel presented him with a new problem. He couldn't be certain who was holding Raul. The CIA, the DEA or possibly even the traitorous Alpha 66 terrorists.

But the old man intended to get him back.

Castro lifted the telephone, pressed the receiver into his ear and punched the intercom to the reception area. Moments later, a tall thin man in a light cotton suit entered the office. Castro noted the cigar in his mouth and the sweet, familiar aroma it sent throughout the room.

"Mr. Premier," the visitor said, extending his hand nervously across the desk.

"General." Castro motioned toward the chair in front of his desk. "I was aware you had arrived. I hope your stay has been enjoyable. My apologies for the delay in seeing you. It has been a most . . . unusual period in the People's Revolution."

Montoya took his seat before replying. "Enjoyable, yes. But I'm sure you're aware that we face serious problems."

Castro smiled. How little the man really knew. He watched Montoya in irritation as cigar smoke rose slowly from the Colombian's mouth to the ceiling. "Yes. I understand that an American gangster has rampaged throughout your country attempting to assassinate you." He smiled again with satisfaction as the other man reddened.

"He'll be brought to justice. It's only a matter of time," Montoya said.

"Yes. But until then, you seek asylum in Cuba?"

The crimson face deepened in color. "Yes."

Castro nodded. He watched as Montoya puffed nervously on the cigar and fought a sudden impulse to rip it from the man's mouth. Then, unable to resist one last insult, he said, "Where you will be safe from harm?"

Montoya looked at the floor. "Yes."

Castro laughed. "You are welcome, of course. For as long as you wish. As a matter of fact, I'm fortunate you have come when you did."

Montoya looked up in surprise. "Please explain."

"I intend to," Castro replied. "Since you and your associates split from Noriega and the Panamanians, it has been difficult to keep our association from the eyes of the world."

"Yes," Montoya agreed, his head bobbing. "But we were both aware there would be problems. We have handled each situation as we encountered it, and we have both grown wealthy in the process."

Castro felt the pain in his chest return as he stared at the greedy man before him. His lips curled into a snarl. "Don't judge me by your standards, Montoya. I haven't done what I have done for personal gain."

"I didn't mean to imply—"

"My navy will escort your shipments for two reasons, and two only. The revenue will help lighten the load of our economic problems." He paused, taking a deep breath, as the hatred threatened to consume him. "And I will delight in knowing that the cocaine will bring misery to the American pigs."

Montoya said nothing.

"But now, I face a most serious problem."

The general leaned forward. "Can I be of some assistance?"

Castro smiled. "I'm glad you have asked. My minister of defense has been kidnapped."

Montoya jerked forward in his chair. "But I understood he was at the resort at La Paz," he said. "How could—"

"It doesn't matter," Castro interrupted. "He's in the hands of the Americans, even as we speak. He was taken from your resort. And it is *you* I hold responsible." He paused to let it sink in.

Montoya stared at him. His hands began to tremble in his lap. "But—"

Castro waved a hand in front of his face. "Don't concern yourself," he said. "I have already made arrangements for his return. The Americans will deliver Raul to the island this evening, but they're demanding a trade." He watched in amusement as a frown spread over Montoya's face.

"A trade? For what?" the Colombian asked.

"You."

The dictator watched the color drain from Montoya's face. He smiled with satisfaction as the man dropped the cigar into the ashtray, reached into his coat pocket and swallowed several tablets from a small medicine bottle.

"You must relax. Rest assured that I have no intention of turning you over to the Americans." The blood slowly returned to Montoya's face. "They have agreed to make the exchange at Bahía de Nipe tonight. There will be no more than two men who come ashore with Raul. It should be a simple enough matter to kill the men who bring him. You'll be along simply as—how do the Americans say it?—window dressing." He stood to indicate that the meeting was over.

Juan Montoya rose from his chair and extended his hand across the desk. Castro gripped the hand and smiled. "Don't worry, my friend," he said. "I'll never allow American agents to operate on Cuban soil. They won't take you from the island against your will."

The hearty odor of Montoya's cigar lingered on after the Colombian had left the office. Castro inhaled deeply, his eyes falling on the key to the desk drawer.

One cigar, he thought. One cigar to celebrate the return of Raul Castillo. One cigar couldn't possibly make any difference.

He inserted the key into the lock, slid open the drawer and withdrew a sealed wooden box.

Perhaps there was still a chance to save his country. He would begin escorting the cartel shipments as soon as Raul was safely back in Cuba. The association with the Colombians would bring millions of dollars to the island.

The old man used the key to break the seal on the box. He lifted a long, thin cigar to his nose and inhaled the aroma lovingly.

Assisting the cartel would also further the second phase of the vision he had held over the years. It would erode the United States from within by sending previously unheard of quantities of cocaine flooding into the country.

The old man placed the cigar reverently between his lips. He smiled as the faintly salty taste of the rolled leaves met his tongue. He reached across the desktop for the lighter he hadn't used in three years.

One cigar to celebrate the return of his friend and the downfall of the American pigs, and to hell with what the doctors said.

Holding the lighter below the tip of the cigar, he spun the wheel with his thumb and gazed into the bluish-yellow flame.

Then slamming the lighter violently against the wall, he gripped the cigar in both hands and snapped it in two.

Castro rose from behind the desk with a new vigor coursing through his body. He crossed the room to the window.

No. Nothing would stand in his way. Not kidnappers, not self-interested weaklings like Montoya and certainly not his health. *Nothing* would prevent his witnessing the destruction of the country that was responsible for the poverty he saw in the streets below.

Fidel Castro extended both arms through the open window. Crumbling the two halves of the cigar between his hands, he released the leaves into the gentle breeze and watched them float softly down to the dirty street.

He turned once more to the photograph of Nikita Khrushchev on the wall.

"We will bury them," he told his old friend.

13

It was time for war.

Bolan unzipped the front of the black night-fighter suit, worked the elastic belt around his waist and secured the Velcro ends. He dropped the small reel-to-reel recorder and the body transmitter into the pockets at the front.

The Executioner lifted the canvas knapsack. The leather straps bit down into his shoulders as he positioned the heavy contents at the center of his back. His eyes fell to the flat plastic rectangles on the couch. A series of numbered buttons extended from the face of each, making them look vaguely like television remote controls.

They *were* remote controls, but the "show" the buttons would tune in if pressed would be far more spectacular than anything the networks had ever produced.

Bolan slid the Beretta's shoulder rig over the backpack straps and holstered the Desert Eagle on his hip. He glanced at the mini-Uzi and magazine carriers that lay next to the controls.

He had no need for them, not on this mission.

The warrior picked up one of the controls and pushed a series of numbers, his efforts causing a small red light to flicker in the corner of the display panel. Satisfied, he dropped the control in the breast pocket of his combat suit.

Raul Castillo stared up at him from his seat at the stateroom desk. The Cuban's lips curled into an amused grin. "And what are you carrying in your bag?" he asked cockily. "A snack? Perhaps we can all have a moonlight picnic on the beach. I hope my premier doesn't forget the wine." He threw back his head and laughed.

Bolan didn't bother to comment. He thought briefly of the many good men—and one woman—who had given their lives in the quest to return the loudmouthed Cuban to his country. A sudden knock on the stateroom door roused him from his thoughts.

The Executioner's hand flashed instinctively to the Desert Eagle. Since the incident in the motor whaleboat, he hadn't left Raul's side. Though there had been no more attempts on the Cuban's life as they sailed through the night, the Executioner would take no chances. Not at this stage of the game.

Bolan cracked the door, pressing the barrel of the big .44 against the metal frame where it could penetrate the barrier and eliminate any threat that might appear on the other side.

Jesse Oven stood in the passageway, flanked by Edwards and Hronopulos.

Bolan glanced behind the three men before swinging open the door and allowing them to enter.

Oven wore a desert cammo uniform, festooned with ammunition belts for the Stoner M63A1 cradled in his arms. Bolan saw that the SEAL lieutenant had replaced the stainless steel Python with a mat-black Sig-Sauer automatic. The heavy 9 mm pistol and a series of double-stacked magazine carriers hung from the web belt around the man's waist.

Bolan locked the door behind them.

"It's almost 1815," Oven said. "All ready?"

The warrior nodded. He turned to Hronopulos and handed the big Greek the second remote control. "You know what to do."

Hronopulos nodded, then shook his head and grinned. "Pollock," he said, "you've gotta have gonads the size of basketballs."

Bolan led the way down the passageway and up onto the bridge, the Beretta held close to his side. When they reached the captain's gig, Edwards extended his hand. "Good luck. We'll plan on seeing you back here later tonight."

"Count on it," Bolan said as the gig descended to the dark waters below.

Oven joined the two sailors near the bow while Bolan and the Cuban took seats in the cabin. The Executioner sat sideways, letting the heavy backpack rest on the back of the seat next to him as the boat cruised through the sea at a steady twenty knots.

Castillo broke the silence. "You're quite skillful at your job, Pollock," he said. "I know no other man, on your side or ours, who could have gotten me safely through the terrorists as you have done."

When Bolan didn't answer, the Cuban pressed on.

"Exactly who *do* you work for?"

The Executioner paused. "America," he finally said.

"Yes, of course," Castillo said. "But are you a CIA operative? Or Drug Enforcement? It's obvious that you're not with the Navy." He studied the Executioner's face. "It's not important. I would like to make you a proposition."

The Executioner knew what was coming. "You'll be wasting your breath."

"Perhaps. Perhaps not. I'll take over the People's Republic of Cuba upon Fidel's death—which I will confide in you—will not be far off."

"You're sure of that, are you?" Bolan said.

"Oh, yes." Castillo laughed. "There's no one else qualified to replace him, particularly now that we have rid ourselves of Ocha. I'll grieve when Fidel is gone, of course, but death for us all, is inevitable. One must look to the future. Let me get to the point. I will double—no, triple—whatever your country is presently paying you."

Bolan caught himself smiling. His country had paid him, all right. But not in money. The United States had provided him and other Americans with the finest brand of freedom in the history of the human race. There was no way a Communist country like Cuba could ever equal, let alone double or triple, *that* payment.

The Executioner's only reward for the services he rendered was the knowledge that he did his part. He helped to rid the free nations of the world of the constant threat people like Fidel Castro and his cohorts represented to that freedom.

It was the only payment he had ever gotten. It was the only payment he wanted.

He turned to the man in the seat next to him. "We'll be there in a few minutes. Keep your mouth shut the rest of the trip. When we tie off at the pier, you do exactly what I tell you to do until I've left the island. Anything out of line gets you dropped where you stand."

The corners of Castillo's mouth curled downward. "You'll never leave the island alive, *yanqui* pig."

The Executioner looked him in the eye. "That's a distinct possibility," he said slowly. "But if I don't, you'll never live to see another day."

Through the darkness of the Gulf of Mexico's night waters, they saw the faint glow of a flashlight as they neared the shore.

THE COXSWAIN CUT the engines and the boat glided alongside the pier. Oven joined Bolan and the Cuban outside the cabin as the bow hook tossed up his line. A lone soldier, AK-47 slung over his shoulder, caught the line and secured it around a cleat.

The three men stepped ashore as the soldier tied off the stern line before turning to face them.

Bolan gazed past him at the sand that separated them from the sixty-foot cliffs. Both the beach and the rocks beyond looked deserted. It didn't matter. The Executioner didn't have to see them. He could feel their presence.

The Cuban raised the flashlight, focusing the beam first on Castillo, then Bolan and finally Oven. He stared at the machine gun in the SEAL lieutenant's hands and shook his head.

Oven glanced toward Bolan. The Executioner nodded, and Oven tossed the Stoner back on board.

"Uno," the Cuban soldier said.

"What the hell does he mean?" Oven asked.

Bolan looked at the soldier who held up his index finger in irritation. "One man only," he said, glancing from Oven back to Bolan.

"That'd be me," Bolan said.

"Now wait just a goddamn minute," Oven protested, stepping toward the man.

The soldier raised the AK-47 and jammed the barrel into Oven's chest. Above the gentle sounds of the surf, Bolan heard the click as the weapon's safety kicked off.

Oven stared the Cuban soldier in the eye. "Well, shit," he finally said. He turned to Bolan. "And I know better than to waste my time arguing with *you*." He swung back on board the gig. "Be careful."

The soldier turned the AK to Bolan. "Your weapons," he ordered in Spanish.

The Executioner slid the Desert Eagle from his hip and thumbed the hammer. He extended his arm and aimed the barrel at the bridge of the soldier's nose. "Enough is enough," he said. For a moment, the two men's eyes drilled holes through each other, then the Cuban's gaze fell to the gaping half-inch hole in the end of the automag. He lowered the AK-47.

Slowly Bolan returned the Desert Eagle to his holster.

The muscles in the soldier's face relaxed and he shrugged. "It won't matter," he said. He turned from the pier and motioned for them to follow.

Bolan grasped Castillo by the arm and led him across the sand to a narrow trail leading into the cliffs.

They followed the soldier up the rugged, winding footpath, stepping over rocks and the stumps of long-dead trees in the scant moonlight. Twice the Executioner had to turn sideways, scraping the bulky backpack along the rock as he squeezed his way through the narrow passage.

Unidentifiable shadows moved in the cliffs overhead, and Bolan heard muffled whispers over the rustling breeze that flowed through the stony corridor.

The warrior pulled the gasping Castillo the last few feet to the top. The Cuban soldier paused to let him catch his breath.

Bolan surveyed the area as best he could in the semi-darkness. The trail widened into a road as it left the cliffs. Dark, dry sugar cane stalks grew from the fields on either side, and down the road, he could make out the lines of what appeared to be an old, colonial-style manor house. Bolan heard the soldier whisper something into the darkness ahead.

Suddenly the sugar cane field bursts into flame.

Castillo jumped under the Executioner's grip. "It's the season for burning the stalks," he said with a sneer, "and I see that Fidel has timed it to honor your arrival."

Bolan and the Cuban followed the soldier down the road, the flames forming a blazing tunnel around them.

As they approached the house, Bolan saw that a carefully manicured four-foot hedge surrounded the yard. Three shadowy figures stepped from the porch and crossed the lawn to meet them as they neared.

The graying beard and faded green fatigues of the man in the lead betrayed his identity.

"Ah," Castillo said as their feet hit the crushed oyster shells of the circular drive. "We're almost home, Pollock."

The mixed scents of bougainvillea, night-blooming jasmine and smoke from the fields filled the Executioner's nostrils. Still holding the Cuban by the arm, he escorted the little man to the middle of the yard and stopped directly in front of Fidel Castro.

Shadows from the nearby inferno skipped across the face of the aging dictator as he eyed the Executioner.

Bolan looked past Castro to the other two men. One wore the uniform of a Cuban general, the grips of a Czech CZ-75 automatic extending from the top of the black patent leather holster on his belt. The third man was Juan Montoya.

The Colombian general shifted his feet nervously as Castro embraced his friend, kissing him on both cheeks. "You were treated well?" he asked him in Spanish.

"Satisfactorily," Castillo replied. He turned to Bolan. "If not for this man, the terrorists would have killed me."

Castro nodded, his face an eerie mixture of lines and shadows in the firelight. "Yes," he said. "It's a shame, then, that he must die."

Castillo agreed. "Yes. I have offered him a position with the Revolution, but he refused."

Bolan unzipped the front of his combat suit to reveal the body transmitter. "We're being monitored," he told Castro.

The words had barely left his mouth when the ship's horn of the *M. E. Hart* sounded in the distance.

Castro burst into laughter. Then the laughter turned to sputters as he bent forward in a sudden coughing fit. The Cuban general held out a handkerchief, but the old man pushed it away, spitting phlegm into the grass at his feet.

The dictator's eyes narrowed, the pupils barely visible under the heavy lids as he regained control. He turned back to Bolan and raised a hand.

Cuban soldiers sprang up from behind the hedges on both sides of the yard. Bolan heard the bolts of a hundred AK-47s slam home as the men fixed their sights on him. Three uniformed snipers appeared on the roof of the house, aiming their night scopes down at the Executioner.

The Cuban premier smiled. "It doesn't matter," he said, reaching behind him and pulling Montoya to his side. "I have given this man my word that you will not take him. And while it doesn't bother me to break an agreement with imperialistic pigs, my word is my bond when dealing with friends." He bent slightly at the waist, leaning closer to the transmitter in Bolan's belt. "Your rescuers will never reach you in time."

"My 'rescuer' is already here," Bolan said. Dropping one arm from the shoulder strap, he swung the backpack around to his chest before setting it on the grass at Castro's feet. Dancing flames reflected off the shiny metal as he unzipped the canvas cover.

Castro's eyes widened, the whites gleaming as he recognized the object.

"You're familiar with the SADM, I imagine," Bolan said. "That's the Special Atomic Demolition Munition. Commonly called the 'backpack' nuke. It's not big—at least not as nuclear weapons go. About half a kiloton. But I can promise you it'll get rid of the cane stalks a lot faster than your fires." Bolan pulled the control from his pocket and held it up for Castro to see in the firelight. "The warhead's only fifty-six pounds," he continued. "I doubt it will reach Havana, so there'll still be something left for whoever takes your place." He paused, watching hatred replace the sudden fear that had overtaken Castro's face.

The old man turned to the soldiers on the roof. "Evaristo," he called to one of the snipers. "Can you hit the correct part of the American swine's brain to prevent his finger from pushing the button as he dies?"

"Yes, sir," came a voice from the roof. "Easily from here. It's in my cross hairs now. I wait only your order."

Montoya laughed. "It seems your bluff is about to be called," he said to Bolan. "Are you certain you are prepared to die?"

Bolan shrugged. "For years, now, Montoya. How about you?" He watched as Montoya chewed on his bottom lip, leaning back slightly, away from the bomb.

The Executioner turned back to Castro. "Tell your man on the roof to go ahead," he said. "But a second after he pulls the trigger, the bomb will be detonated from the ship, and this end of Cuba will join Atlantis somewhere at the bottom of the sea."

The ship's horn answered again, the slow, haunting sound drifting across the waves of the Bahía de Nipe.

The veins in Castro's neck stood out as blood raced to his face, transforming it into a loathsome, grotesque mask. He turned to the general, ripped the CZ-75 from his holster and shoved the barrel toward Bolan.

"I have given Juan Montoya my word that you will not take him from Cuba against his will," he screamed into the warrior's face.

Then slowly, the dictator's features softened, and a grin began to break around the corners of his mouth. Draping his left arm around Montoya's shoulders, he said, "And I will keep my promise."

Montoya smiled weakly. "Thank you, my friend," he said.

Castro nodded.

Then in one sudden movement, he grabbed Montoya's hair, shoved the gun under the Colombian's chin and fired.

The speeding 9 mm round entered Montoya's throat and traveled up into the brain, exiting through the top of his skull.

"You're welcome," Castro replied.

The man who had been the leader of one of the most powerful drug cartels fell forward onto the grass, the crown of his head a mass of bone fragments and blood.

Fidel Castro coughed, spit phlegm onto Montoya's body and turned to Bolan. "American agents will never operate on Cuban soil," he said, his face a savage veil of fury. He draped an arm around Raul's shoulders and turned away.

Bolan watched as the raging old man, his friend and the general walked back toward the house.

Castro stopped abruptly as he reached the porch. Slowly he turned back to face the Executioner. "In the words of an old comrade," he said. "'We will bury you.'"

Bolan stared at the gray-bearded dictator who stood framed by the other two men, his eyes glowing embers of hatred as hot as the fires of hell.

"Don't count on it," the Executioner told him.

Throwing the backpack over his shoulders, Bolan made his way between the walls of fire to the cliffs.

The head of the most ruthless drug smuggling organization in the world was dead. The deaths of Janie, the members of the SEAL team, and the others who had died in the process had been avenged.

But Mack Bolan harbored no misconceptions about the future of the cocaine trade. The Colombians would reorganize. Someone would rise to take the place of the fallen king.

The white plague of cocaine that ate at the very soul of America had been slowed—not eradicated, Bolan knew, as he made his way back down the cliffs to the beach.

There would be more wars, and more lives would be given before the drug problem was stamped out.

It wouldn't just disappear.

But neither would the Executioner.

A breakaway faction of NATO plots to "free" Europe from the superpowers.

THE BARRABAS SWEEP

JACK HILD

The Realm, a murderous faction of NATO powered by a covert network of intelligence, paramilitary and corporate empires across Europe, proposes to liberate the continent from NATO. It's an infallible plan designed for destruction — until ex-Special Forces colonel Nile Barrabas and his crack commando squad step in.

Phoenix Force—bonded in secrecy to avenge the acts of terrorists everywhere

SEARCH AND DESTROY $3.95 ☐
American "killer" mercenaries are involved in a KGB plot to overthrow the government of a South Pacific island. The American President, anxious to preserve his country's image and not disturb the precarious position of the island nation's government, sends in the experts—Phoenix Force—to prevent a coup.

FIRE STORM $3.95 ☐
An international peace conference turns into open warfare when terrorists kidnap the American President and the premier of the USSR at a summit meeting. As a last desperate measure Phoenix Force is brought in—for if demands are not met, a plutonium core device is set to explode.

Total Amount	$ _____
Plus 75¢ Postage	_____ .75
Payment enclosed	$ _____

TAKE 'EM NOW

FOLDING SUNGLASSES
FROM GOLD EAGLE

Mean up your act with these tough, street-smart shades. Practical, too, because they fold 3 times into a handy, zip-up polyurethane pouch that fits neatly into your pocket. Rugged metal frame. Scratch-resistant acrylic lenses. Best of all, they can be yours for only $6.99.

MAIL YOUR ORDER TODAY.

Send your name, address, and zip code, along with a check or money order for just $6.99 + .75¢ for postage and handling (for a total of $7.74) payable to Gold Eagle Reader Service. (New York and Iowa residents please add applicable sales tax.)

Remove from pouch   unfold once   unfold twice   and they're ready to wear

 GOLD EAGLE Gold Eagle Reader Service
901 Fuhrmann Blvd.
P.O. Box 1396
Buffalo, N.Y. 14240-1396

GES-1A

Offer not available in Canada.

ABLE TEAM®

DICK STIVERS

Action writhes in the reader's own streets as Able Team's Carl "Ironman" Lyons, Pol Blancanales and Gadgets Schwarz make triple trouble in blazing war. Join Dick Stivers's Able Team—the country's finest tactical neutralization squad in an era of urban terror and unbridled crime.

"Able Team will go anywhere, do anything, in order to complete their mission. Plenty of action! Recommended!"
—*West Coast Review of Books*

AT-1R-A

Do you know a real hero?

At Gold Eagle Books we know that heroes are not just fictional. Everyday someone somewhere is performing a selfless task, risking his or her own life without expectation of reward.

Gold Eagle would like to recognize America's local heroes by publishing their stories. If you know a true to life hero (that person might even be you) we'd like to hear about him or her. In 150-200 words tell us about a heroic deed you witnessed or experienced. Once a month, we'll select a local hero and award him or her with national recognition by printing his or her story on the inside back cover of THE EXECUTIONER series, and the ABLE TEAM, PHOENIX FORCE and/or VIETNAM: GROUND ZERO series.

Send your name, address, zip or postal code, along with your story of 150-200 words (and a photograph of the hero if possible), and mail to:

LOCAL HEROES AWARD
Gold Eagle Books
225 Duncan Mill Road
Don Mills, Ontario
M3B 3K9
Canada

HERO-1R